Grandpa
Talks about God

Michael S.
Lawson

CF4·K

 ISBN: 1-84550-250-7; 978-1-84550-250-8

Published by Christian Focus Publications
Geanies House, Fearn, Tain, Ross-shire,
IV20 1TW, Scotland, UK.
www.christianfocus.com

Cover illustration: Kim Shaw Inside illustrations: Kim Shaw

Cover design: Danie van Straaten

Printed and bound by Bell and Bain, Glasgow

Scripture verses quoted are from the New International Version and the International Children's Bible (New Century Version) unless otherwise stated.

Dedication

For seventeen years, the children of Metropolitan Baptist Church inspired me to think more clearly about God. We worked together in Junior Church to study about and worship Him. I dedicate this book to those children who were so patient with me during those years.

My two grandchildren, Meridee Paige and Benjamin Shannon Lawson, have renewed my sense of wonder about God and His works. I dedicate this book to them and my deepest desire is that they along with all the children of the world would come to love the God of the Bible.

I want to thank God Himself for all the lessons He taught me along the way before He would let me write about Him in this way.

Michael S. Lawson

God is

A letter for you...

Hi there kids!

Hummingbirds dart around the glass feeder outside my window as I write these words. I love hummingbirds. In one way, these wonderful little birds help grow my love for the God who created them.

The God of the Bible loved you and me before we were born. He wants us to love Him too! Loving God is the most important thing we do every day.

In this book there are thirty-five words which begin to describe God. I did not make these up. They are found in the Bible. These thirty-five words do not tell you everything about God but they tell you some important things.

I hope you enjoy the stories which explain each word. The story is the first of five parts to help you explore how that word describes God. In fact, you could take one part each weekday and still be thinking about that same word. If you do, you will learn a little about God every weekday for thirty-five weeks.

I do hope everything in this book helps you love God more. He deserves to be at the center of your life. He is the most wonderful person you will ever meet. He is waiting for you.

Grandpa Mike

Each lesson includes a fun, illustrated story to read as well as the following sections to help you understand what Grandpa Mike is telling you about God.

Where is this found in the Bible?

Summary

Why is this important?

Something to do

Something to think about

1. God is Adorable

What do you say when you see baby animals? "Oh, they're so cute." But your mother probably says, "Oh, they're just adorable." My wife must have said something similar when she saw two baby ducks. Anyway she brought them home. I named them "Peep" and "Poop" based upon what they seemed to do the most ... peeping and pooping! I have to admit they were adorable.

At first, we kept them in the garage. We put them in a small box with a light to keep them warm. As they got bigger, we gave them a large shallow container of water. They loved it! They made such a mess! We decided to move them outside to our fenced porch. The weather was warm and the porch seemed an ideal place.

"Peep" and "Poop" never made friends with us. They ran every time we came on the porch. One day, "Poop" squeezed through a crack in the fence and hid under the porch. My son was the only one small enough to crawl under the porch and quick enough to catch little "Poop". Finally we released them on the lake behind our house. They seemed glad to get off the porch. Everyone was happy to see them paddling in the lake. I think I was the happiest of all since I hated cleaning up after little "Poop". But when they were little, they were adorable.

God is adorable. The Bible tells us to love God with all our heart. That is what adorable really means. Would it be strange to adore little ducks so much and God so little? Our main response to God ought to be adoration. The second verse of one old and famous hymn begins like this, "Holy, Holy, Holy, all the saints adore thee."

God is adorable. He is much more adorable than two little ducks. Do you feel that way about God?

Where is this found in the Bible?

Let those who love the LORD hate evil, for he guards the lives of his faithful ones and delivers them from the hand of the wicked (Psalm 97:10).

Because I love your commands more than gold, more than pure gold, and because I consider all your precepts right, I hate every wrong path (Psalm 119:127-128).

"'Love the Lord your God with all your heart and with all your soul and with all your mind.' This is the first and greatest commandment. And the second is like it: 'Love your neighbor as yourself.' All the Law and the Prophets hang on these two commandments" (Matthew 22:37-40).

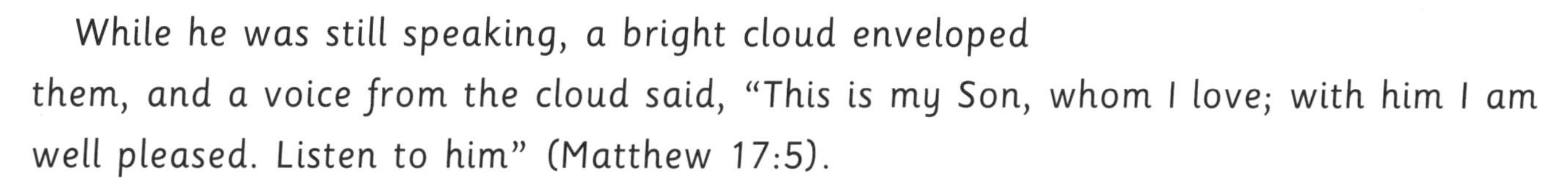

While he was still speaking, a bright cloud enveloped them, and a voice from the cloud said, "This is my Son, whom I love; with him I am well pleased. Listen to him" (Matthew 17:5).

Read Deuteronomy 10:12-13 and John 14:30-31

Summary:

1. Adoring God should be our basic response to God (Deuteronomy 10).
2. Adoring God means we hate evil (Psalm 97).
3. Adoring God means loving his commands (Psalm 119).
4. Jesus taught us to adore God (Matthew 22).
5. Jesus Himself adored God and showed it by obedience (John 14).
6. Jesus was adored by the Father (Matthew 17).

Why is this Important?

God wants to give and receive love. He adores His children. He expects them to adore Him. He is our Heavenly Father.

The natural response of a baby to a loving parent is to love them back. The baby learns to love their parent more and more. Even now, you probably love your parents more than you did when you were younger. You are just beginning to learn how much they love you and how much they have done for you. Our first and most natural response to God should be to love Him. God knows that the more we come to know Him the more we will adore Him. That is why He wants us to learn about Him in the Bible. In the Bible, we discover God's tenderness, gentleness, and mercy. We find out how He let his own Son die so we might live with Him forever. Each truth we learn about God should fill our hearts with more love for Him.

God wants us to love those things He loves and hate those things He hates. The more we do that, the more we become like Him. Little by little our love for God makes us more like Him.

We must never forget that Jesus came to remind us about this basic message. He clearly taught us to adore God the Father in Matthew 22. Jesus wanted the world to know that He Himself loved God the Father and willingly did whatever the Father told Him to do in John 14. That is why God the Father speaks from heaven in Matthew 17 to tell anyone who would listen how much He loves His Son.

God invites us to come to know Him. You can know how wonderful God is for yourself. When you do, you will realize, "God is adorable."

Something to Do:

Find something you love very much. Hold it in your hands. This can be a favorite toy, blanket, or animal. Now, think about how hard it would be to give this to your worst enemy. Think how you would feel if your enemy tore up your toy or killed your pet. Do I love God as much?

Go and find the toy you wanted the most from last Christmas. Hold it in your hands. Remember how you felt two days before Christmas when you were hoping you would get it? Do you feel the same way about God?

Now, each time you pick it up this week, think about how much you love God for letting you use such a wonderful thing. Keep a score sheet like this: "1111" with each mark indicating how many times you thought about God. How many times did you handle the toy and think about God this week?

Something to Think About:

- Why is it easier to love creatures rather than the creator?
- In what ways have you loved God with your heart? Mind? Body?
- Can you think of new ways to love God with your heart? Mind? Body?
- When you look at a baby animal can you begin to think about how wonderful the God who created him is?

2. God is Angry

Making Mom angry was not a good idea. If you made her angry, justice was quick and certain. Her rules were simple:

1. Don't lie.
2. Do exactly what she said right now.
3. Never use a disrespectful tone of voice.

I kept those rules most of the time. But one night while everyone was at the dinner table I looked at the food and said, "What is THAT"? My tone of voice broke rule Number 3. I don't know why I used that tone of voice. Sometimes I did dumb things. This was one of them. Mom was really angry. She excused me from the table without any dinner. In fact, she excused me for several nights.

When I got older, I understood why Mom got angry. Oh sure, she made mistakes. Most parents do once in awhile. They normally feel bad later. But Mom wanted me to be a good person. She knew if I broke her simple rules good people would not want to be my friends. Life would be harder. When I broke her rules, she always disciplined me.

God is like that. God wants me to be good. He is angry when I lie or break His rules. He calls it sin. God sees every wrong and it makes Him angry. He knows breaking His rules will make my life worse not better.

God should punish me for each wrong thing I've done. If He did, I would never see Him again. I would have to live with other mean selfish evil people forever. So, God let Jesus take my punishment. Jesus was punished for each wrong thing I have done. The Bible says, "He (Jesus) is the atoning sacrifice for our sins, and not only for ours but also for the sins of the whole world" (I John 2:2).

With Mom, I had to pay for my own sins. Unlike God, her punishment only lasted a few days. Soon I was eating dinner with the family again. I never used that tone of voice again. I learned how much I liked eating dinner with the family.

Where is this found in the Bible?

You alone are to be feared. Who can stand before you when you are angry? (Psalm 76:7).

But the LORD is the true God; he is the living God, the eternal King. When he is angry, the earth trembles; the nations cannot endure his wrath (Jeremiah 10:10).

"'The LORD is slow to anger, abounding in love and forgiving sin and rebellion. Yet he does not leave the guilty unpunished; he punishes the children for the sin of the fathers to the third and fourth generation.' In accordance with your great love, forgive the sin of these people, just as you have pardoned them from the time they left Egypt until now" (Numbers 14:18,19).

Who is a God like you, who pardons sin and forgives the transgression of the remnant of his inheritance? You do not stay angry forever but delight to show mercy. You will again have compassion on us; you will tread our sins underfoot and hurl all our iniquities into the depths of the sea (Micah 7:18,19).

Read Isaiah 12: 1-2 and Isaiah 34:1-2

Summary:

The Bible describes God's anger in these different verses:

1. He is angry with everyone who disobeys or resists Him (Isaiah 34).
2. The whole earth shakes when He is angry (Jeremiah 10).
3. He alone is to be feared since no one can handle his anger (Psalm 76).
4. He is slow to anger (Numbers 14).
5. He does not stay angry forever but delights to show mercy (Micah 7).
6. One who asked for forgiveness received comfort instead of anger (Isaiah 12).

Why is this Important?

We live in a world full of right things and wrong things. I wish I would naturally choose right instead of wrong but it just isn't true. I have chosen wrong things enough to know I often prefer the wrong thing. I need to know that God gets angry when I do something wrong. That helps me want to choose right instead of wrong.

In the story, my Mom got angry when I broke her rule. Her anger let me know what she thought was bad. The same is true with God. I would not know what He thought was bad unless He told me what made Him angry.

God and Mom got angry for the same reason. God wants the best for me and others around me. God is angry when I sin. God knows that sin destroys me from the inside. Sometimes sin works quickly. More often, sin works slowly. I become less and less concerned about God and more and more concerned about myself. Sometimes I say to myself, "God does not know what is best for me. I know what is best for me." Then I know I am in trouble.

There are many more reasons for God's anger than we have discussed in this short section. God's anger lets me know we must choose how we will meet God. We can receive His justice, which means He will punish us for our own sins. Or, we can receive His mercy, which means we will accept Jesus' punishment for our sins.

I like four things about God's anger: God gets angry very slowly; God does not stay angry forever; God satisfied His anger by punishing Jesus instead of me; God prefers to show mercy and eagerly forgives any who ask Him for it.

Something to Do:

The next time you feel angry count to the number ten to see if you can stop yourself from losing your temper. What things make you angry? Would you be angry if your mum blamed you for something your brother or sister had done? Would you be angry if you were punished instead of them? Take the words, 'The Lord is slow to anger, abounding in love.' Underneath the word slow draw something that is slow such as a snail or an old car. Underneath the word abounding draw a pile of expensive looking presents or a rich treasure chest. This should remind you about how patient and loving God is.

Something to Think About:

- Do you get angry slowly or quickly? Why?
- Do you forgive people when they say they are sorry? Why? Why not?
- Would you take a punishment for a friend if they got in trouble?
- What is the worst punishment you can think of? Remember that Jesus took the worst punishment for you.
- What would you like to say to Jesus when you see Him face to face? Would you like to tell Him right now in a prayer?

3. God is Beautiful

Our vacation in Colorado was just about over. Before sunup the big Pontiac roared to life and began rumbling east toward Texas. This time I was awake. For some reason, Mom let me sit in the front seat. In Texas we call that seat "shotgun". The second man on old stage coaches would protect the coach with his shotgun. Dad and I talked quietly about the things we enjoyed the most on vacation.

I loved Colorado and so did Dad. I loved the smell of pine and sage, the sound of running water, the feel of cool dry air and the taste of food cooked on an open fire. My Dad did not believe you had been on vacation if you did not go to Colorado. He loved the majestic mountain peaks. He taught me to love them too.

Then it happened. Dad said simply, "Look!" The sun was beginning to peep above the horizon. I had never seen the sun rise before. Normally I slept in the back seat until breakfast. "How many colors do you see?" Dad spoke in awe.

He spoke slowly, "Did you ever wonder why we always begin so early?" "Well, yes", I replied. "I don't want to miss the sunrise." He paused then whispered, "Each one is so beautiful and different. No one can paint a sunrise. No one can capture it in a photograph. Paintings and pictures are always too small. A true sunrise fills the whole sky. It is living beauty. Every minute the scene changes slightly. New colors come and others fade away. You have to experience the beauty of a sunrise." Dad taught me something wonderful about himself and God.

Only a beautiful God would think to make something so beautiful to start every day. I never forgot that lesson. One day we will see just how beautiful God really is. Until then, we can simply enjoy what He has created.

Where is this found in the Bible?

In that day the LORD Almighty will be a glorious crown, a beautiful wreath for the remnant of his people (Isaiah 28:5).

One thing I ask of the LORD, this is what I seek: that I may dwell in the house of the LORD all the days of my life, to gaze upon the beauty of the LORD and to seek him in his temple (Psalm 27:4).

He has made everything beautiful in its time. He has also set eternity in the hearts of men; yet they cannot fathom what God has done from beginning to end (Ecclesiastes 3:11).

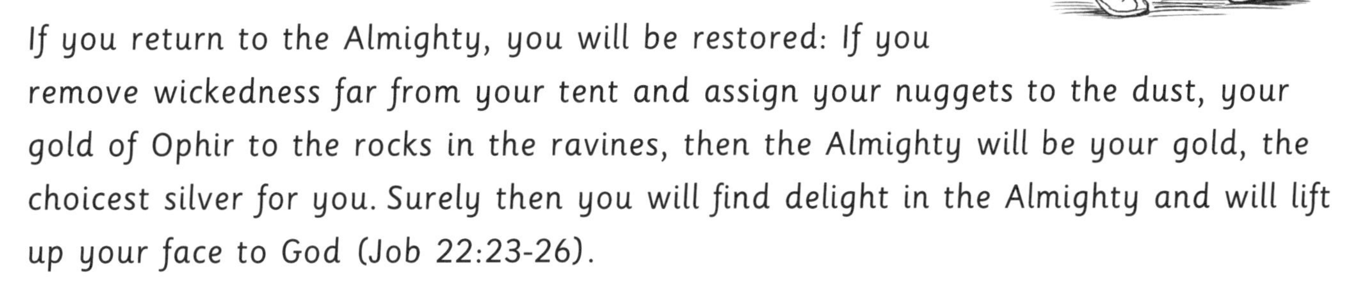

If you return to the Almighty, you will be restored: If you remove wickedness far from your tent and assign your nuggets to the dust, your gold of Ophir to the rocks in the ravines, then the Almighty will be your gold, the choicest silver for you. Surely then you will find delight in the Almighty and will lift up your face to God (Job 22:23-26).

This is what the LORD says: "Heaven is my throne, and the earth is my footstool. Where is the house you will build for me? Where will my resting place be? Has not my hand made all these things, and so they came into being?" declares the LORD (Isaiah 66:1-2).

If he were on earth, he would not be a priest, for there are already men who offer the gifts prescribed by the law. They serve at a sanctuary that is a copy and shadow of what is in heaven. This is why Moses was warned when he was about to build the tabernacle: "See to it that you make everything according to the pattern shown you on the mountain" (Hebrews 8:4-5).

Read I Chronicles 22; 29:11-13 and II Chronicles 9

Summary:

1. The people of Israel will see God as beautiful (Isaiah 28).
2. The psalmist longs to spend eternity studying God's beauty (Psalm 27).
3. One of Job's friends declares how delightful God is to the pure of heart (Job 22).
4. David gave 3 billion dollars worth of gold to build God's temple (I Chronicles 22).
5. The tabernacle sanctuary was just a shadow of heaven (Hebrews 8).
6. All wealth comes from God (I Chronicles 29).
7. God asks those who try to impress Him, "Has not my hand created all these things?" (Isaiah 66).

Why is this Important?

I am naturally drawn to beautiful things, aren't you? I like beautiful things made by God and man. In the story I was learning to love sunrises. I also learned to love sunsets, flowers, butterflies, birds, mountains, streams and all the beautiful things God has made.

His work impresses me. For instance, I have seen a gold nugget as big as a basketball. I've seen a bucket full of uncut diamonds each one as big as your thumb.

Man can take God's creation and fashion beautiful things as well. I have seen jewelry made from gold, paintings of sunsets, bouquets of flowers, and clothing made from birds' feathers. All were beautifully man-made using God's creation.

God created us to love beautiful things because He is beautiful. How can we know that God is beautiful? Yes, two of the verses you read simply tell us He is beautiful. We can also look at what God made. God's creation is a product of His character. God wants us to look past the beautiful things we see and believe they come from His beautiful character. He wants us to be drawn to His beauty.

In the verses you read it says that the tabernacle was just a shadow of the beautiful heavenly tabernacle. Even the temple built by Solomon which began with 3 billion dollars worth of gold is smaller than God's footstool which is the earth.

God is beautiful, more beautiful than I can even imagine.

Something to Do:

Find the most beautiful thing in your home or family. Create a sign that says: "This reminds me of God who is very beautiful." Decorate the sign the very best you know how. Now, with care, place the sign near the beautiful thing you chose.

Something to Think About:

- What does it mean to "be beautiful on the outside but ugly on the inside?"
- If you spent as much time making your inside as beautiful as your outside, how much time would you spend each day?
- If you could make your inside beautiful, would you want to?
- How do you think people get beautiful on the inside?

4. God is Colorful

Red, blue, yellow, black, orange, green, purple, and brown, yep, all eight crayons were sharp and ready in my new crayon box. I was eager for school to start and proud of those brand new crayons. Soon I would wear them down and tear the paper partially off. But today they were new and sharp.

I did not know there were bigger boxes with lots more colors. Imagine my surprise when the boy at the next desk pulled out a huge box with colors like "magenta," "aqua", and "hazel". I loved the bigger box at once.

I had my own idea about how to color a great picture. I'd use as many different colors as possible! My teachers encouraged me to choose just a few colors and use them wisely. But their suggestions never slowed me down. If a few colors were good, a lot of colors were better. My pictures had as many colors as I could get my hands on.

Today, colors mostly confuse me. For instance, can you name 256 different colors? Neither can I, but my computer says that I can select from 256 different colors. Scientists tell us that the human eye can distinguish five billion different colors. I suppose someone really ought to give each one a different name, but I'm kind of busy right now, how about you?

Since God invented those colors he'll have a name for every single one. He must be colorful. I think God must love lots of colors just like I do. When I see beautiful colors, I think about how colorful He must be.

Where is this found in the Bible?

And God said, "This is the sign of the covenant I am making between me and you and every living creature with you, a covenant for all generations to come: I have set my rainbow in the clouds, and it will be the sign of the covenant between me and the earth. Whenever I bring clouds over the earth and the rainbow appears in the clouds, I will remember my covenant between me and you and all living creatures of every kind. Never again will the waters become a flood to destroy all life. Whenever the rainbow appears in the clouds, I will see it and remember the everlasting covenant between God and all living creatures of every kind on the earth" (Genesis 9:12-16).

Then there came a voice from above the expanse over their heads as they stood with lowered wings. Above the expanse over their heads was what looked like a throne of sapphire, and high above on the throne was a figure like that of a man. I saw that from what appeared to be his waist up he looked like glowing metal, as if full of fire, and that from there down he looked like fire; and brilliant light surrounded him. Like the appearance of a rainbow in the clouds on a rainy day, so was the radiance around him. This was the appearance of the likeness of the glory of the LORD. When I saw it, I fell facedown, and I heard the voice of one speaking (Ezekiel 1:25-28).

Read Revelation 4: 1-3

Summary:

The Bible doesn't specifically say God is colorful. We know God is colorful because He created light and the rainbow. The rainbow breaks light down into the visible color spectrum. So the rainbow displays all the colors.

1. God uses His personal rainbow to publicly remind us of His promise (Genesis 9).
2. Ezekiel sees God's radiance and it was just like a rainbow (Ezekiel 1).
3. Almost 700 years later, the Apostle John sees a rainbow around God's throne (Revelation 4).
4. John describes God as appearing like variously colored stones. Jasper was clear like a diamond and carnelian was red like a ruby (Revelation 4:3).

Why is this Important?

Imagine for just a minute that God told us we could see heaven every Thursday from 4:00 to 4:15? You simply turn your television to Channel 3,

each Thursday and glimpse heaven. In one way, He has done exactly that by creating our world full of color. How could anyone so colorful be boring? When we look at our world, we see a little bit of what heaven and the presence of God must be like – full of colors that dazzle the eyes.

1. How could God's creation be more colorful and interesting than He is? The fact that He is colorful lets me know He is exciting. God fills the earth with color. He painted each sunrise and decorates each butterfly.

2. Every description of heaven in the Bible uses color. God surrounds Himself with color. Nothing about God is boring including the colors that fill the heavens and the earth.

3. Some people think heaven will be boring. I think God is going to let us work with all the wonderful colors He created. How could that possibly be boring? Just imagine a crayon box with every color God created.

Something to Do:

• Color a picture and make sure you use a color different from the normal appearance. For example, purple - grass, green - sky, etc.

• Look out one window – and write down all the colors you see. Challenge someone in your family to find a color not on your list.

• Hawaiians have several different names for blue just so they can describe precisely the various tones they see in the ocean. Go to the paint section of your nearest department store. Ask for a color chart for blue. Can you think up original names for each "blue" on the chart?

Something to Think About:

• Do you think heaven is more colorful or less colorful than earth?

• Why do you think God created such a colorful place for us to live in?

• What if God let you decorate the world with any colors you wished? What color would the grass be? What color would you make the leaves? Should the ocean still be blue? How about the sky? Perhaps you could use colors that do not have names yet. Do you love the fact that God is colorful?

5. God is Creative

Have you ever thought about unusual (exceptional) living creatures? One scientist carefully studied the rules we use to build airplanes. Then he applied those rules to bumble bees. His precise mathematical calculation proved bumble bees cannot fly. Their little wings cannot support their bulky bodies. I'm glad bumble bees do not read mathematical studies. I like the ones that visit my flowers in the front yard.

That study made me think of other unusual birds in God's world. Of course, everyone knows that birds fly. So why does the penguin swim and the ostrich run? Neither of those birds can fly.

Can you think of fish that don't swim? Neither can I! But I can think of fish that do more than swim. One salt water fish flies and one fresh water fish crawls. Okay, the flying fish only flies a short distance but that's still further than I can fly. And crawl? Yes, there is a South American catfish that crawls to another pond when his pond dries up. He can breathe for a considerable period of time.

Can you think of some exceptional mammals? The kangaroo hops around on two legs instead of four. The whale lives in the sea instead of on land. I know a squirrel that flies instead of jumping from tree to tree.

Chameleons change body color. Ants manage teamwork better than humans. Silk worms create soft threads that make fine fabrics. Lightning bugs create light in their tiny bodies.

Wow! How did God think of all these living creatures? God must have a wonderful imagination. I would say He is creative!

Where is this found in the Bible?

In the beginning God created the heavens and the earth (Genesis 1:1).

Remember your Creator in the days of your youth, before the days of trouble come and the years approach when you will say, "I find no pleasure in them" (Ecclesiastes 12:1).

For you created my inmost being; you knit me together in my mother's womb. I praise you because I am fearfully and wonderfully made; your works are wonderful, I know that full well (Psalm 139:13-14).

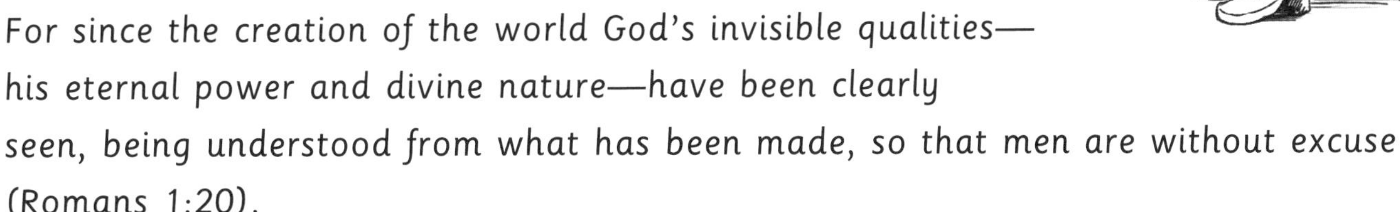

For since the creation of the world God's invisible qualities—his eternal power and divine nature—have been clearly seen, being understood from what has been made, so that men are without excuse (Romans 1:20).

Read Isaiah 40:28 and Isaiah 65:17-18

Summary:

1. God created the heavens and the earth (Genesis 1).
2. Young men and women are urged to remember God (Ecclesiastes 12).
3. God's creation shows He has unlimited energy and strength (Isaiah 40:9).
4. God's creation shows He has understanding beyond human wisdom (Isaiah 40).
5. God created each human personally (Psalm 139).
6. We can know some things about God by studying His creation (Romans 1).

Why is this Important?

The more I know about God's creation the more I admire how wonderful He is. His creation stirs my imagination.

What He created fascinates me. Everywhere I look His creative work surrounds me. Whether I look through a telescope or a microscope His creation impresses me.

God wants us to see His character through His creation. If we find His creation fascinating, we will be more impressed by His character. He reveals some things about His character in the creation. He reveals even more about His character in the Bible. It is good to fall in love with God's character.

God's creativity affects how I think about myself. The Bible tells me I am created in His image. That explains why I sometimes feel creative and enjoy trying new and different things.

Many people find ways to express the creative image they bear from God. They paint pictures, invent gadgets, construct buildings, write poetry and compose music, among other things. Yet the most creative things man ever invented only copy what God made in the beginning.

I can always learn more about God by learning more about the heavens and the earth. I can also learn more about God by reading what He wants me to know about Himself in the Bible. There will always be something new to explore. Every time I look at something new I will remember, "God is creative!"

Something to Do:

- Write down ways someone in your home has been creative with words, colors, music, or other resources.
- Look in your yard and write down how someone has been creative with plants, structures, or substances. Look at the design and color of just one insect - for example a butterfly.
- Be creative yourself. Do some painting, singing, write a poem, build with some lego. Now think about how wonderful God is and how wonderful it is to be creative like Him.
- Create a new melody for a favorite song.
- Take a picture frame and put colored paper in it. Hang it in your room.

Something to Think About:

- How does creation (sun, moon, stars etc.) show us God's power?
- What parts of the creation make you think most about God?
- Do you look at creation without thinking about God who created it? Why?
- In the new heavens and the new earth, what 10 things would you most like God to create or fix? Why?
- Which colors do you like best and why?
- Are you impressed with words, colors, sounds that God has placed in His world?
- Because God is creative He can solve perplexing problems.
- Because God is creative He is enjoyable to get to know.
- Because God is creative He helps me to understand myself because I am created in His image.
- Because God is creative that means He enjoys diversity.
- Because God is creative that means that God's rules must make sense.

6. God is Everywhere

I loved to play in the little creek close to our house. That creek had so many busy things swimming around. Tadpoles, tiny frogs and swarms of minnows begged me to chase them up and down the creek.

My friend Lance had a Mr. Science microscope. One day we put a drop of the water under that microscope. Wow! The water came alive with creepy critters whose names I never knew.

Lance's family lived next to the creek. His parents built a swimming pool between the house and the creek. Now that pool presented a real problem for me. The only thing I liked better than playing in the creek was swimming in the pool. Why did I have to choose? Why couldn't I be in two places at the same time?

Life would have been perfect if I could have played in the creek and swam in the pool at the same time. Today I wish I could be in two places at the same time more than ever.

God lives like that all the time. He is in two places at once. In fact, He is everywhere at the same time. I do not really know how He does that. I sure feel better knowing that He is everywhere. That means I can never get far away from God. He is always near because He is everywhere.

Where is this found in the Bible?

"Am I only a God nearby," declares the LORD, "and not a God far away? Can anyone hide in secret places so that I cannot see him?" declares the LORD. "Do not I fill heaven and earth?" declares the LORD (Jeremiah 23:23-24).

"The God who made the world and everything in it is the Lord of heaven and earth and does not live in temples built by hands. And he is not served by human hands, as if he needed anything, because he himself gives all men life and breath and everything else. From one man he made every nation of men, that they should inhabit the whole earth; and he determined the times set for them and the exact places where they should live. God did this so that men would seek him and perhaps reach out for him and find him, though he is not far from each one of us. 'For in him we live and move and have our being.' As some of your own poets have said, 'We are his offspring.' (Acts 17:24-28)

Read Psalm 139: 7-12

Summary:

1. God is both near and far away (Jeremiah 23).
2. Jeremiah wonders where a person could hide from the presence of God.
3. Jeremiah explains that God fills both the heavens and the earth.
4. We learn that whether we are high or low, God is there (Psalm 139).
5. We cannot even hide from God in the darkness (Psalm 139).
6. We live in the presence of God (Acts 17).

Why is this Important?

The verses you just read show that God is everywhere. Acts 17 gives the best explanation of God's presence. Paul says all of life is lived in God's presence. We live in God's presence. Everyone lives in God's presence.

Some people live as though God moved far away. Some people live as though God cannot see at night. Do you think they will be surprised or embarrassed when they learn they did everything in God's presence? No one can hide from God. God sees every secret action. No one can escape the presence of God.

I'm glad God is everywhere. When I was younger I worried that I might accidentally go somewhere without God. That is impossible because God is everywhere. In fact, no one can make me go where God is not present. I have met Christians who were put in the world's deepest darkest prison cells. Their guards did not know God was there too!

I also worried about whether God could see me at night. Sometimes I would hear noises in the night. I was too young to know if they were real or not. What if something terrible grabbed me? Would God know? Would He see? Now I know that He sees everything because all of life is lived in His presence.

God's presence everywhere gives me confidence to live. I know that God is near me wherever I go. I cannot get far away from God even if I wanted to. So no matter where I go or what happens to me, I know that God is there. Wow! I am really glad God is everywhere.

Something to Do:

Get a picture of the night sky. Put Jeremiah 24:23 at the bottom of the picture. Now go outside, look at the stars and think about God being every where in the heavens. Look at a globe of the world. Put a tiny dot near the place where you live. Think about all the other people who live in your dot. Remember all the people in every dot live in the presence of God. Are you glad God is everywhere?

Something to Think About:

- If you could be in 5 places at the same time, where would you be and what would you be doing?
- If you could visit any place in the Universe, where would it be? And what would you hope to see?
- Have you ever wished God was not everywhere? Why?
- Have you ever been glad God was everywhere? Why?
- Name one place you're glad that God is right now.
- God can see everything (both good and bad).
- I cannot accidentally get where God cannot reach me. I cannot even get away on purpose.

7. God is Fair

I was terrified. They wanted me to umpire!

My brother-in-law lived in Iowa and played in a softball league. He invited me to watch him play. That sounded like fun until no umpires showed up. Suddenly everyone was looking at me! I was terrified!

Umpires made me laugh. I remembered all the terrible things people said about umpires. Some people have more fun booing the umpire than watching the game. No matter what they do, somebody thinks the umpire is wrong. I sure did not want to be one.

Both teams really wanted to play. They could not play without an umpire. I became their unwilling victim. Each side promised not to argue about any bad call. They wouldn't let me say "no." The best umpires make bad calls from time to time but I made them most of the time. Being absolutely fair all the time is just about impossible. The game seemed to last forever as I made one terrible call after another.

Both teams kept their promise. No one complained. I was sure glad when that game was over.

Now I appreciate God more. The Bible says that He is judge of all the earth and then asks, "Will not the judge of all the earth do right?" The answer is, "Of course he will." He is absolutely fair. No one will ever be able to accuse Him of not being fair.

Where is this found in the Bible?

Masters, provide your slaves with what is right and fair, because you know that you also have a Master in heaven (Colossians 4:1).

for acquiring a disciplined and prudent life, doing what is right and just and fair; (Proverbs 1:3).

"You came down on Mount Sinai; you spoke to them from heaven. You gave them regulations and laws that are just and right, and decrees and commands that are good" (Nehemiah 9:13).

All this is evidence that God's judgment is right, and as a result you will be counted worthy of the kingdom of God, for which you are suffering. God is just: He will pay back trouble to those who trouble you and give relief to you who are troubled, and to us as well. This will happen when the Lord Jesus is revealed from heaven in blazing fire with his powerful angels. He will punish those who do not know God and do not obey the gospel of our Lord Jesus (II Thessalonians 1:5-8).

Then I heard a loud voice from the temple saying to the seven angels, "Go, pour out the seven bowls of God's wrath on the earth." The first angel went and poured out his bowl on the land, and ugly and painful sores broke out on the people who had the mark of the beast and worshiped his image. The second angel poured out his bowl on the sea, and it turned into blood like that of a dead man, and every living thing in the sea died. The third angel poured out his bowl on the rivers and springs of water, and they became blood. Then I heard the angel in charge of the waters say: "You are just in these judgments, you who are and who were, the Holy One, because you have so judged; for they have shed the blood of your saints and prophets, and you have given them blood to drink as they deserve." And I heard the altar respond: "Yes, Lord God Almighty, true and just are your judgments" (Revelation 16:1-7).

Read Deuteronomy 32:4

Summary

1. Proverbs connects the three words, "right", "just", and "fair".
2. Masters who owned slaves were expected to be fair because their heavenly master (God) is fair with them (Colossians 4).
3. The wise man who imitates God will seek to live a just life (Proverbs 1).
4. Everything God does is just (fair) (Deuteronomy 32).
5. God gave just (fair) laws to Israel (Nehemiah 9).
6. God will deal with every wrong ever committed (II Thessalonians 1).
7. God is completely just (fair) in his judgment of the world (Revelation 16).

Why is this Important?

In the story you just read, the players had a terrible time. They did not know whether to swing the bat or not because I was so inconsistent in my calls. That made the game very difficult for the players. The normal rules for softball were certainly not being observed consistently. I had no one to blame but myself. I made those players miserable.

Imagine what life would be like if God punished people who did wrong, and rewarded those who did good, but not all the time. Or worse, what if God rewarded those who did wrong and punished those who did right sometimes?

In fact, that is just the way life appears. Sometimes good people get punished and bad people get rewarded. Your parents may have said it, "Life just isn't fair". They are correct. Life is not fair. But God is fair. And life may appear to end at death but the Bible tells us there is life after death. In the life after death, God will make everything fair. Life in God's eternal kingdom will be perfectly fair all the time.

What a relief! Because God is fair I do not have to punish or reward those around me. If I was a poor umpire, I would be an even worse judge. Fortunately, God will take care of that. I need to make sure I am living right. If I live right I know one day God will reward my choices and my behavior. I'm really glad God is fair. That helps me love Him more.

Something to Do:

• At school today, make a list of wrong things your classmates do that the teacher does not see. Do not write down any names. Or keep a score card like this: Write on one side the number of times your teacher must correct a student. Write on the other side the number of things you see your classmates do that the teacher should correct but doesn't see. Now at the bottom of the sheet write, "One day, God promises to make everything right."

Something to Think About:

• Would you like to attend a school that was perfectly fair? Why? How would that school be different from the one you attend?

• Have you ever won or lost a game you didn't deserve to win or lose? How did you feel?

• Have you ever wanted to win so much that you were willing to cheat? Why do you think winning is so important?

• What 3 things do you think God will do first when He begins to make everything right again? Do other members of your family have a different list?

8. God is Faithful

Do you like popcorn - fresh, hot and buttery? Imagine having all the popcorn you wanted! As a little boy I did! My dad owned a popcorn company. I can still eat more popcorn than anyone I know.

My dad sold popcorn in several states. He would be at the office before 6:00 a.m. Even on his days off customers would call my dad for more popcorn! "Can't they wait?" I asked. But my dad would always stop what he was doing, get in the car, go to the office, load the popcorn and take it to his customer. When I asked him why, his answer was always the same, "I promised I would bring them popcorn whenever they needed it."

My dad believed in promises. "Be a man of your word" he told me. That meant, "If you make a promise, keep it!" Everybody knew my dad kept his promises.

God is like that. He always keeps his promises. That's what the Bible means by "faithful". The Bible gives many examples of promises God made and kept.

Where Is It Found in the Bible?

The Bible describes many promises from God. Here are two. A long time ago, people were so bad that God destroyed the world with a flood. God's flood covered the whole world. Only eight people lived. God promised He would never destroy the world with a flood again. He put a rainbow in the sky to remind everyone of His promise. You can read the whole story in Genesis 6 - 9.

Some time later, the Jewish people were slaves in Egypt. God promised to free them. God performed many miracles to do this. The last miracle helped the Jewish people cross the Red Sea on dry land. The Egyptian army chased them and thought they could cross the Red Sea too but God drowned the whole army. He kept his promise to free the Jewish people. Sounds impossible? That's why it's a miracle. You can read this for yourself in Exodus 3 - 14.

Summary:

Here are just a few promises that God makes for today: He promises to forgive our sins. He promises to give Eternal life to anyone who believes in Jesus. He promises to answer prayer. He promises to reward those who seek Him.

He promises to work everything for good to those who love Him.

Here are two of God's promises about the future: He will destroy the whole world, this time with fire not a flood. He has prepared a special place for everyone who loves Him. Remember, God is faithful. He always keeps His promises.

Why is this Important?

Can you think of something that does not depend on God's promises and faithfulness? I cannot. If God were to break even one promise we could never trust Him again. We would always wonder if he was going to keep or break a promise.

God wants us to trust Him. We can trust Him because He is faithful. We can believe that He forgives our sins. We can believe that He answers prayer. We can believe He will destroy and rebuild the world.

I love knowing God is faithful. I feel safe! Life may be hard now. I may become ill or even die, but God is faithful. He keeps His promises to you and me.

Something to Do:

Tell your parents that for a whole week you will: Keep your room tidy; Always say "please and thank you"; Brush your teeth every morning and every night; Pray before you go to sleep. At the end of the week discuss with your parents: Did you break any promises? Which ones? How many times? Which ones were the hardest to remember? How hard would these be if you had to keep them for a month? A year? Were there times when you were sorry you made those promises? Can you imagine God remembering and keeping hundreds of promises for thousands of years? Are you glad God is faithful?

Something to Think About

- Do you have any favorite promises from God and can you find them in the Bible?
- Have you ever prayed, "Thank you God for keeping your promises"?
- Do you love God more now that you know He is faithful? Why?
- Do you love God more than popcorn? I do!

9. God is Famous

"Please get in the limousine", the driver said. Wow, my first ride in a limousine! The next day I was meeting with a hotel executive to discuss some business. They impressed me by sending a limousine to pick me up at the airport.

I was wearing a cowboy hat and boots so I looked just like a country music star! My dark glasses protected my eyes from the glaring winter sun. I was enjoying the ride from the airport to the hotel and hoped the driver would go very slowly. I was in no hurry for this ride to end. At first I didn't notice. Then I began to watch as cars slowed down when they passed us. Some even shadowed us for quite a long time. Why were the people looking over at the limousine? Car after car did the same thing.

Then it dawned on me! I was in Nashville, the home of Country Music. All these people thought I was a famous country music star. The windows of the limousine were tinted so people could not see me clearly. I decided to have some real fun.

I waved at the next car that slowed down to look inside the limo. They got very excited and waved back. I've always wondered who they thought I was. All the way to the hotel, I pretended I was a famous country music star. But then I wondered, wouldn't it be wonderful if people were as excited to see God as they were to see a famous music star? God is a lot more famous than a music star.

Where is this found in the Bible?

"I will set a sign among them, and I will send some of those who survive to the nations—to Tarshish, to the Libyans and Lydians *(famous as archers)*, to Tubal and Greece, and to the distant islands that have not heard of my fame or seen my glory. They will proclaim my glory among the nations" (Isaiah 66:19).

But Joshua asked, "Who are you and where do you come from?" They answered: "Your servants have come from a very distant country because of the fame of the LORD your God. For we have heard reports of him: all that he did in Egypt, and all that he did to the two kings of the Amorites east of the Jordan—Sihon king of Heshbon, and Og king of Bashan, who reigned in Ashtaroth (Joshua 9:8-10).

LORD, I have heard of your fame; I stand in awe of your deeds, O LORD. Renew them in our day, in our time make them known; in wrath remember mercy (Habakkuk 3:2).

For by now I could have stretched out my hand and struck you and your people with a plague that would have wiped you off the earth. But I have raised you up for this very purpose, that I might show you my power and that my name might be proclaimed in all the earth (Exodus 9:15-16).

For your Maker is your husband— the LORD Almighty is his name— the Holy One of Israel is your Redeemer; he is called the God of all the earth (Isaiah 54:5).

It does not, therefore, depend on man's desire or effort, but on God's mercy. For the Scripture says to Pharaoh: "I raised you up for this very purpose, that I might display my power in you and that my name might be proclaimed in all the earth" (Romans 9:16-17).

Read Psalm 102:12 and Romans 1: 19-21

Summary:

1. From the creation of the world, people have known about God (Romans 1).
2. People choose to ignore God though they know about Him (Romans 1).
3. God sends missionaries so everyone hears the truth about God (Isaiah 66).
4. The Gibeonites heard about the God who worked miracles in Egypt (Joshua 9).
5. Hundreds of years later Habakkuk explains that he has heard of God's fame (Habakkuk 6).
6. Isaiah calls Him God of all the earth (Isaiah 54).
7. Exodus 9 tells how God used Pharaoh to publicize His name to all the earth.

Why is this Important?

There are about 6,000 different languages in the world. Each one has a name for God. No one has ever discovered a language without a name for God. Some languages have even more than one name. One scholar lists over 150 different names for God in the Bible.

There are some famous people in the world. American presidents and movie stars are famous around the world. But none of them is as famous as God.

Even if everyone in the world knew George Washington's name, he would not be as famous as God. People have known about God ever since the world began. So God is not just famous now. He has been famous for thousands of years.

Just because you have a name for God does not mean you know the truth about God. Some people know very little about God. Some people make up stories about God. Some people have crazy ideas about God. Some people say God lives in kumquats and butterflies, every plant and animal. Some people say God doesn't live on earth at all. But everyone knows at least one name for God. That makes Him the most famous person of all.

I wish people would let God tell them what He is like instead of making things up. God tells us what He is like in the Bible. By the way, the Bible is the most famous book in the world. The Bible has been translated into more languages than any other book. More copies of the Bible have been printed than any other book. Don't you think the most famous person should be written about in the most famous book? Me too!

Something to Do:

- Can you think of a different famous person before Jesus, after Jesus and today? Can you think of anyone besides God who has been famous for more than 4,000 years? Would they have been famous with every group of people all around the world?

Something to Think About:

- Are non-famous people as important as famous people? Why?
- Would you like to have a famous person's autograph? If so, whose would you like? Why? Would you like to read a story about their life? What questions would you like to ask them?
- If you wanted to be famous, what could you do to make sure everyone knew your name?
- Do you know God personally? Are you glad to know the most famous person in the whole world? What more would you like to know about Him? What questions would you like to ask Him?

10. A New Best Friend

You have just read about the character of God. Did you learn some amazing things? Now I'm going to explain how to be friends with God.

You may know something about friends. In fact, you might even have a friend. Do you and your friend talk to each other? Do you like to play together? Have you ever wondered how God could be your friend? God wants to be your friend. He is a good friend because he will always be with you and will always do what is best for you. I will tell you how God can be your best friend after I tell you how being friends with God got started.

A long time ago, God created the world and everything in it. He created huge mountains, deep oceans, amazing animals and beautiful plants. He also created a man and a woman. Their names were Adam and Eve. God and Adam and Eve were best friends. God gave them a special garden to live in. God gave them all the delicious fruits and healthy vegetables they could eat. Best of all, God talked with Adam and Eve every day. God loved Adam and Eve very much. He gave them everything they needed. There was only one rule that God gave Adam and Eve. They were not to eat from one tree in the beautiful garden where they lived. They could eat from every tree except that one.

One day Adam and Eve disobeyed God and ate the fruit from the forbidden tree. God was very sad. Adam and Eve were ashamed. When Adam and Eve disobeyed God, sin came into the world. God calls disobedience sin. Because of sin, the world wasn't perfect any more. Worse of all, Adam and Eve were not best friends with God any longer. God cannot be best friends with anyone who has sin.

Now, because Adam and Eve sinned, everyone is born with sin. Sin makes our hearts look dirty to God. Sin separates us from God. He is absolutely clean and nothing dirty can be close to Him. Since every person's heart is dirty, we can't be friends with God. We show that we have sin when we are mean to our brothers or sisters; when we don't tell the truth; when we take something that doesn't belong to us. Those things make God sad.

Even though God was sad when Adam and Eve sinned, He still wanted to be friends with them. He wants to be friends with you. In fact, He wants everyone to talk to Him and spend time with Him. God wanted people to always be His best friends. So He decided to send someone special to make a new friendship possible. God didn't want our hearts to be dirty anymore. He sent someone who could make them clean. The only one who could make our hearts clean was someone just like God. So God sent His son to earth and His name is Jesus.

Jesus had a mom and dad who raised Him while He was here on earth. He grew up and did lots of fun and exciting things just like you do. When He was a grown up He taught about His Heavenly Father, God. He performed many miracles to prove He was God's Son. Some people didn't like Him because He said He was God. So they killed Him. But God raised Jesus back to life on the third day. Jesus' death and coming back to life was in God's plan.

Here is the great part, Jesus died so our hearts wouldn't have to be dirty anymore. Jesus' death means your heart can be clean and we can be friends with God again. If you know your heart is dirty and believe that Jesus died for you to make it clean, He will wash your heart and make it clean like His. Now, if your heart is clean you can talk to God and spend time with God just like Adam and Eve did before they sinned. God can be your very best friend. Jesus made it possible to be friends with God. Do you want to be His friend?

Ask Jesus to wash your heart. Ask God to start being your best friend. Here are some verses that will help you remember that your heart is dirty, but Jesus will wash it clean.

Where is this found in the Bible?

All people have sinned and are not good enough for God's glory (Romans 3:23 NCV).

If you use your mouth to say "Jesus is Lord" and if you believe in your heart that God raised Jesus from death, then you will be saved. We believe with our hearts, and so we are made right with God. And, we use our mouth to say that we believe, and so we are saved (Romans 10:9-10 NCV).

Jesus is the way our sins are taken away. And Jesus is the way that all people can have their sins taken away, too (I John 2:2 NCV).

We have been made right with God because of our faith. So we have peace with God through our Lord Jesus Christ. Through our faith, Christ has brought us into that blessing of God's grace that we now enjoy. And, we are happy because of the hope we have of sharing God's glory (Romans 5:1-2 NCV).

11. God is Generous

Aunt Teetse and Aunt Dodie came often to our home. My mother's two sisters had very different lives. Aunt Teetse worked in a bank and wore flashy clothes, jewelry and expensive perfume.

Aunt Dodie lived a more simple life. She wore plain clothes and almost no make up. She lived in a remote mountain cabin and survived on government checks because both her husbands died early in life.

I loved Aunt Teetse's visits. She always bought expensive and unusual gifts. One time she took me to buy a new pair of Sunday shoes. She drove me to the most expensive store in town. My mother never shopped there. We could have bought shoes for half as much anywhere else. I really took good care of those shoes.

I loved Aunt Dodie's visits too. She always cooked special food. If I close my eyes and concentrate, I can still taste her enchiladas, chicken and dumplings, and crab gumbo. Aunt Dodie always had time to play dominoes or cards. I will always remember she taught me how to fish. Aunt Dodie was generous with her time.

God is like that. God is generous. He gave his most expensive gift so we could live with Him forever. He gave His son to die for our sins. I cannot think of anything more precious. If we believe His son died for our sins, He gives us eternal life with Him. Eternal is a long time.

Where is that found in the Bible?

"For God so loved the world that he gave his one and only Son, that whoever believes in him shall not perish but have eternal life" (John 3:16).

If any of you lacks wisdom, he should ask God, who gives generously to all without finding fault, and it will be given to him (James 1:5).

But when the kindness and love of God our Savior appeared, he saved us, not because of righteous things we had done, but because of his mercy. He saved us through the washing of rebirth and renewal by the Holy Spirit, whom he poured out on us generously through Jesus Christ our Savior, so that, having been justified by his grace, we might become heirs having the hope of eternal life (Titus 3:4-7).

Read 2 Corinthians 9:6-7

Summary:

1. Nothing has more value than the life of your only child and God gave his one and only Son (John 3).
2. God generously gives wisdom to any who ask (James 1). (Look this passage up in your own Bible to find out the conditions).
3. God generously gives the Holy Spirit to those whom He saves (Titus 3).
4. God loves His children to be as generous as He is (2 Corinthians 9).

Why is this Important?

In the beginning, Adam and Eve created a problem. They disobeyed God. They needed to pay for their disobedience. How could they pay God? What would they give Him? He owns all the gold and diamonds. He owns everything. So Adam and Eve had a problem. If they could not pay the debt, they could not live in heaven. They were in deep trouble.

In the story you just read both my aunts gave generously to me in different ways. They were generous because I was their nephew. Since Adam and Eve were God's children, we might expect God to be generous with them.

God was generous. He willingly gave His most precious gift to help them. I don't know anyone except God who would be willing to give their only child to pay the debt for ungrateful people. Fortunately, God is generous. God solved this problem.

When Adam and Eve disobeyed God, they did not just create a problem for themselves. They created a problem for all of us. They passed their sin down to us. Now we need God to be generous with us. I have wonderful news. God loves to be generous.

The Bible says, "He (Jesus) is the atoning sacrifice for our sins, and not only for ours but also for the sins of the whole world" (I John 2:2). Are you grateful for his generous gift?

Something to Do:

- Take your favorite toy and sit it in the middle of the floor, or if it's small, on a table.
- Discuss with your mom or dad what it would feel like to give it away to some child at the Homeless Mission.
- How will you feel if the child does not want your gift?
- How will you feel if the child does not say 'thank you' for the gift?

Something to Think About:

- Think about God's gift. Eternal life with Him means:

  No more sickness or death.

  No more sadness or tears.

  No more mean or dangerous people.

  Plenty to eat and drink.

  An endless variety of things to see and do.

  Heaven is better than your best dream.
- Will I see you there?

12. God is Gentle

"Did you see it?" my daughter said. "See what?" I answered.

The summer mountain day sparkled. Everyone walked in high spirits. I crossed the small wooden bridge over the bubbling mountain stream last. On the other side, everyone was asking "Did you see it?"

"See what?" I answered.

"The nest!" Their eyes flashed their excitement.

"A bird's nest? On the bridge?" I asked.

"No! In the tree! A little hummingbird has built her nest there!"

I had to go back. I had never seen a hummingbird's nest. I looked and looked at the small pine branch on the tree next to the bridge.

Finally I saw the little bird sitting on her tiny nest. She sat motionless. She didn't even blink. She covered and warmed the baby eggs with her body. The eggs were no bigger than the fingernail on your baby finger. The day we saw the eggs everyone just stared.

Each day we came back to the bridge. We paused only briefly to look at the amazing little bird on her tiny nest. One day when the mother was gone, our eyes almost popped out. We saw three teeny-tiny babies snuggled in the little nest.

I tried to imagine teeny little hearts and lungs inside those babies. Every wee organ had to work perfectly or the baby would die. I really wanted to pick one up.

But the slightest pressure between my fingers would obviously damage the fragile baby bird.

Later I thought God created these baby birds. He made each tiny part of these wonderful babies. If God made them, He could pick them up if He wanted to. God is gentle. God, so big, so powerful, but gentle enough to handle a baby hummingbird. I'm still amazed at how gentle God is.

Where is this found in the Bible?

After the earthquake came a fire, but the LORD was not in the fire. And after the fire came a gentle whisper (1 Kings 19:12).

Rejoice greatly, O Daughter of Zion! Shout, Daughter of Jerusalem! See, your king comes to you, righteous and having salvation, gentle and riding on a donkey, on a colt, the foal of a donkey (Zechariah 9:9).

Take my yoke upon you and learn from me, for I am gentle and humble in heart, and you will find rest for your souls (Matthew 11:29).

By the meekness and gentleness of Christ, I appeal to you—I, Paul, who am "timid" when face to face with you, but "bold" when away (2 Corinthians 10:1).

Read Matthew 21:5

Summary:

1. God spoke to Elijah in a gentle voice in 1 Kings 19.
2. Zechariah predicted that God's messiah will be gentle in chapter 9.
3. Matthew tells us that Jesus came as the gentle messiah in chapters 11 and 21.
4. Paul tries to persuade the Corinthians based upon the gentleness of Christ in 2 Corinthians 10.

Why is this Important?

In the story the little hummingbird babies would not want me to pick them up. Even if I was very careful, I could easily cause some permanent damage.

So what would happen if God picked us up in His hands? Perhaps we think that someone so big could hurt us? Will God crush us when He deals with us?

Jesus taught His disciples in John 10 that they were in his hand and he was in the Father's hand. Here is what He said "My sheep, (Jesus describes us as sheep) listen to my voice; I know them, and they follow me. I give them eternal life, and they shall never perish; no one can snatch them out of my hand. My Father, who has given them to me, is greater than all; no one can snatch them out of my Father's hand. I and the Father are one" (John 10:27-30).

Being in the father's hand could be dangerous unless God is gentle. The Father's hand could easily crush us. So I'm glad the Bible tells us God is gentle.

If I really believe God will be gentle with me, I feel safe. I want to get close to Him even if I have done something wrong. I read in the Bible how gently God deals with those who have sinned but come asking for help and forgiveness.

Something to Do:

- Try to peel a grape without bruising the flesh of the fruit. (Ask your Mom or Dad to help you).
- Fry an egg and turn it over without breaking the yoke. (Ask your Mom or Dad to help you).
- Is it hard work to be gentle?

Something to Think About:

- How gentle would you need to be to fix the wing of a butterfly?
- Why do we think that someone big may not be gentle?
- What story in the Bible best shows God's gentleness in your opinion?
- Who is the gentlest person you know? When you see this person again, will you think about God?
- The story of the thief on the cross impresses me. He hung dying on that cross because he had stolen someone else's property. Jesus was dying too, but He spoke gently. He promised the thief they would enter paradise together that very day. You can read this story in Luke 23:26-43.

13. God is Holy

I never really liked shoes. I loved bare feet and summer tar bubbles. The street in front of my home contained a wonderful mixture of tar and gravel. Summertime in Texas gets really hot. The tar would bubble up and I would pop the tar bubbles with my big toe. Fun! All summer long I played barefoot except for Sunday.

Every Sunday I had to put on my Sunday shoes. Does your mother have special Sunday shoes for you? My mother made me keep my best shoes just for Sunday.

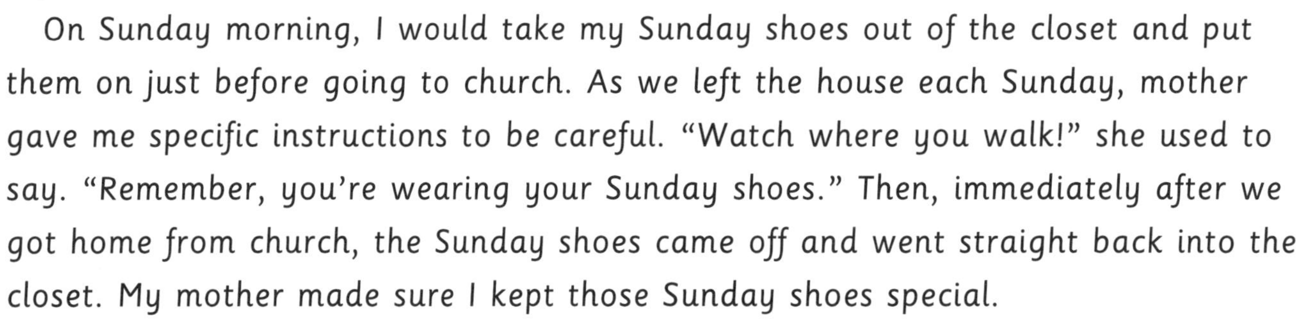

On Sunday morning, I would take my Sunday shoes out of the closet and put them on just before going to church. As we left the house each Sunday, mother gave me specific instructions to be careful. "Watch where you walk!" she used to say. "Remember, you're wearing your Sunday shoes." Then, immediately after we got home from church, the Sunday shoes came off and went straight back into the closet. My mother made sure I kept those Sunday shoes special.

As I said, I never liked shoes - especially Sunday shoes. I never wore out a pair of Sunday shoes. I never walked in mud puddles or popped tar bubbles with them. They always looked brand new even when they no longer fit my feet.

I did learn that Sunday shoes were special. They were not like other shoes. Sunday shoes were just for church and treated with special care. In one way, that is what it means to be "holy." Something that is holy is set apart for a special purpose. It is also unique - unlike anything else. But we know that this perfect, flawless and pure God is all of these things and so much more.

God is "holy". He requires us to treat Him in a special way.

Where is this found in the Bible?

"There is no one holy like the LORD; there is no one besides you; there is no Rock like our God" (1 Samuel 2:2).

In the year that King Uzziah died, I saw the Lord seated on a throne, high and exalted, and the train of his robe filled the temple. Above him were seraphs, each with six wings: With two wings they covered their faces, with two they covered their feet, and with two they were flying. And they were calling to one another: "Holy, Holy, Holy is the LORD Almighty; the whole earth is full of his glory" (Isaiah 6:1).

As obedient children, do not conform to the evil desires you had when you lived in ignorance. But just as he who called you is holy, so be holy in all you do; for it is written: "Be holy, because I am holy" (1 Peter 1:14-16).

I am the LORD who brought you up out of Egypt to be your God; therefore be holy, because I am holy (Leviticus 11:45).

Read Revelation 4:8 and 15:3-4

Summary:

1. God alone is holy according to Revelation 15 and I Samuel 2.
2. Isaiah 6 and Revelation 4 describe heavenly beings who declare, "Holy, Holy, Holy" as they look at God.
3. Leviticus 11 and 1 Peter 1 tell us to be Holy because God is Holy.

(Each of these ideas is presented in both Old and New Testaments.)

Why is this Important?

In the story you just read, my Sunday shoes were different from my other shoes. God is different from humans. If God were human or just a "super-human" then He would not be worthy of worship. God is different from humans because He is full of everything good and completely empty of evil. Just like my Sunday shoes had no mud or tar on them, God has no evil in Him. He is Holy.

God is different from the angels or any heavenly creature. They fly around God's throne saying, "Holy, Holy, Holy". Neither angels nor heavenly creatures can compare to God. God alone is Holy.

My Sunday shoes had to be treated differently. I could only wear them on Sunday. I had to give them special care. I put them in the closet where they would not get dirty. God must be treated differently. That is why the heavenly beings fear Him (Psalm 89). That is why Habakkuk tells the earth to be quiet (Habakkuk 2:20). God is Holy and He lives in His Holy Temple. He must be treated with utmost admiration and respect.

Six times in the Bible God says, "Be holy for I am Holy." God wants us to be Holy. God wants us to be different just like He is different. God wants us to be full of everything good just like He is full of everything good. God wants us to be free from evil just like He is free from evil.

I am glad God is Holy. I pray that He will help me be holy.

Something to Do:

- Can you find something special in your home that you can only use on special occasions? Is there something in your house that only your Mom and Dad are allowed to touch because it is so precious? Ask someone at home why this thing is special.

Something to Think About:

- If we treat objects with such special care, how should we treat God?
- Do you think you will treat God differently when you see Him face to face?
- What kinds of things do you think you will do differently?
- Should you start to do any of those things right away?
- What should someone do for God to show how special He is?

14. God is Huge

I had been asked to teach some children about God. I wanted to compare God's size with human size. I needed an example.

First, I thought about ants. Would God be as big as a human is to an ant? That did not seem big enough. Then I thought about germs. Would God be as big as a human is to a germ? I did not like germs. Plus, pretending people were germs did not sound good to me.

I decided to fill a huge glass bowl with sand. I told the children each piece of sand was like one star in space. One grain of sand somewhere inside that bowl would be our sun. Our sun is not the biggest star but it is not the smallest either.

The earth would be like an invisible speck of dust floating around that piece of sand. Somewhere on that piece of dust would be our neighbourhood and our Children's Church class. Now imagine a gymnasium filled with bowls of sand. God is bigger than all the bowls while I live on the speck of dust.

God is huge. Even my example does not fully explain God's size. The Bible teaches God's size is without limits. We cannot measure his size. Sometimes I have to remind myself how huge God really is. I look up and imagine his smiling face fills the sky. Of course God is bigger than that but it helps me remember God is huge.

Where is this found in the Bible?

O God of Israel, let your word that you promised your servant David my father come true. "But will God really dwell on earth? The heavens, even the highest heaven, cannot contain you. How much less this temple I have built! (1 Kings 8:26-27).

To the LORD your God belong the heavens, even the highest heavens, the earth and everything in it (Deuteronomy 10:14).

"The temple I am going to build will be great, because our God is greater than all other gods. But who is able to build a temple for him, since the heavens, even the highest heavens, cannot contain him? Who then am I to build a temple for him, except as a place to burn sacrifices before him?" (2 Chronicles 2:5-6).

Read Psalm 113:4

Psalm 139:1-12

For the director of music. Of David. A psalm.

O LORD, you have searched me and you know me.
You know when I sit and when I rise; you perceive my thoughts from afar.
You discern my going out and my lying down; you are familiar with all my ways.
Before a word is on my tongue you know it completely, O LORD.
You hem me in—behind and before; you have laid your hand upon me.
Such knowledge is too wonderful for me, too lofty for me to attain.
Where can I go from your Spirit? Where can I flee from your presence?
If I go up to the heavens, you are there;
If I make my bed in the depths, you are there.
If I rise on the wings of the dawn, if I settle on the far side of the sea,
even there your hand will guide me, your right hand will hold me fast.
If I say, "Surely the darkness will hide me
and the light become night around me,"
even the darkness will not be dark to you;
the night will shine like the day, for darkness is as light to you.

Summary:

1. Moses says that the highest heavens belong to God in Deuteronomy 10.
2. Solomon says that the highest heavens cannot contain God in 1 Kings 8 and 2 Chronicles 2.
3. The psalmist says that God's glory is above the heavens in Psalm 113.
4. David claims there is no place to hide from God's presence in Psalm 139.

Why is this Important?

Humans have always believed in god. Notice I did not capitalize "god". I did that for a reason. The god or gods humans believe in rarely resemble the God of the Bible. They prefer a god big enough to help but small enough to control. They like a god that will do what they want. They do not want a god they must obey. They cannot squeeze the Bible's huge God into their small mind. So people most often picture God a lot smaller than He really is.

In the past, humans created idols to represent their gods. In some parts of the world men still make idols. None of these gods compare in size with the God revealed in the Bible.

Many people who do not make idols still create a god in their mind. Of course their god always fits what they want. I once asked a lady on an airplane what she thought about hell. She said, "Oh, my god wouldn't send anyone to hell. He loves people." She was half right! "Her god" would not send anyone to hell. But the God of the Bible promises to send some people to hell.

I then asked her why she believed that. She said, "I just believe it!" In other words she made up a god who fit her mind. At some point in life we have to decide whether we believe what God revealed about Himself in the Bible, or whether we believe our own imagination. When my idea about God disagrees with what the Bible reveals about God, I should change my idea. God is bigger than my idea.

I'm really glad that God is bigger than my imagination, bigger than everybody's imagination and, bigger than the universe. His size assures me He can control what He has created. I love God because He's huge! If God was not huge, He would have to run around the universe checking on things.

Something to Do:

Here is what you need:

2 cups of sand
Sheet of newspaper
Magnifying glass
Tweezers
Fingernail polish or
Marble, ball bearing or small round stone

Spread the sand on the sheet of paper.
Pick up one grain with the tweezers. (You may need the magnifying glasses).
Paint that one grain of sand with the fingernail polish.
Place the painted grain back in the sand. Imagine you live on the painted grain. Imagine that all the grains represent the universe and God is bigger.
Now read Job 7:17. Do you wonder with Job if God is so big and we are so small why He bothers with us? When you think of God's size, you might want to ask the same question as Job and David.

Something to Think About:

- When you consider God's size are you even more amazed at Jesus' claim that God takes note when even one sparrow falls from the sky and God has numbered the hair on our head?
- If people believed in God and thought about how big he really is, would they be more likely to do what He commands?
- What would you do if you could see how big God is?
- Do you think God is big enough to keep all His promises?

15. God is Invisible

"I can't see God", one little boy said in Sunday school. "How can I be sure God is real?"

Now that's a really good question, I thought. God certainly is invisible. So do I have to see God to believe He's real? "What about the wind?" I said. "You can't see the wind, but you know it's real." "I can feel the wind" the little boy answered. "But I can't feel God." He was asking very good questions. I was not giving very good answers.

Today I think I have a better answer. See if the following answer helps you. I've never seen nor felt my grandfather. He died long before I was born. But I believe he was real. I was told he lived in Fort Worth, Texas, and owned an ice cream factory. I sure wish I could have seen, felt and tasted his ice cream.

My grandfather had three sons and two daughters. One of his sons was my father. He's the one who told me all about my grandfather. So, in one way, my grandfather is invisible. I sure can't see or feel him. But I believe my grandfather was real. I believe my father was telling me the truth. That's how it is with God.

God is invisible. We can't see Him. But those who have seen Him have told us about Him in the Bible. My Dad's brothers and sisters told me the same things about my grandfather. Many different people tell us about God in the Bible. We believe our parents tell us the truth. Yes, God is invisible, but He's also real.

Where is this found in the Bible?

Since the creation of the world God's invisible qualities—his eternal power and divine nature—have been clearly seen, being understood from what has been made, so that men are without excuse (Romans 1:20).

He (Jesus) is the image of the invisible God, the firstborn over all creation (Colossians 1:15).

For by him all things were created: things in heaven and on earth, visible and invisible, whether thrones or powers or rulers or authorities; all things were created by him and for him (Colossians 1:16).

Now to the King eternal, immortal, invisible, the only God, be honor and glory for ever and ever. Amen (1 Timothy 1:17).

Read Hebrews 11:27

Summary:

1. God's invisible qualities can be seen through His creation (Romans 1).
2. Jesus is the visible representation of the invisible God (Colossians 1).
3. Jesus created other invisible beings who have authority and power (Colossians 1).
4. This invisible God should be worshiped and praised forever (1 Timothy).
5. In Hebrews it tells us that Moses saw God. Many Bible scholars believe that He actually saw Jesus before He came to earth as a baby since the Bible also says that no man has seen God at any time. Jesus Himself said, "If you have seen me you have seen the Father."

Why is this Important?

Most of the people in the world believe in invisible beings. Some call them angels. Some call them gods. Some call them demons.

The Bible clearly teaches there are many invisible beings, including God. I don't know much about the invisible beings whirling around our universe, but I know something about God. I am glad that God created and controls both the visible and the invisible things.

The verses above surprise us by teaching that God is both invisible and visible. He is personally invisible. But His invisible qualities can be seen through His creation. Anyone can look at the creation. When anyone looks at the visible world they should believe that a powerful eternal God created everything.

Even more amazing, God came visibly to earth as Jesus. Jesus Himself claimed to be God. Christians agree that a man cannot become god. But the Bible teaches that God became a man. That man was Jesus. Many skeptical people saw Jesus and concluded, "He is God". Jesus even said, "if you have seen me you have seen the Father." Those who saw Jesus saw God.

One day God will be visible to everyone. In that day the Bible says that every person will bow and admit that Jesus is Lord! Even the people who don't believe in invisible things will have to bow to Jesus. Until then, I'm glad God keeps the invisible world under control.

Something to Do:

Collect five or six old magazines. Cut out pictures of things that use invisible things such as: radio waves; microwaves; T.V. remote; infrared waves; electricity. Can you think of others? Paste all the pictures on one sheet of paper. Label your paper "Invisible Things I Believe in". You might want to put God's name on the paper since you won't be able to find a picture of Him

Something to Think About:

- Why are we afraid of things we cannot see?
- When people saw Jesus, why do you think they did not believe He was God?
- The Bible says we were created in the image of God. When we look at one another, what should we think about God?
- If most of the world is right about invisible creatures, are you glad God is one of them?
- Do you believe He is able to control them?

16. God is Joy

I never made friends with winter. I love being warm and dry. Winter brought wet and cold. My family moved to Missouri when I was three and back to Texas when I was five. The memory of two Missouri winters still makes me shiver.

During those winters I had to stay inside most of the time. When I did go outside, I couldn't stay very long. My feet got cold. I could never keep them as warm as summer. Those winters made me love warm weather.

The first birds to arrive as the weather got warm were the robins. I watched them hop around our yard looking for bugs. The first flowers I saw in the spring were dandelions. Their bright yellow blooms brought a smile to my face. Robins and dandelions brought joy to the last gloomy days of winter and the first warm days of spring.

God is better than robins or dandelions. God is full of joy. God brings joy! God is joy. Real joy lives deep within God's character. He shares His joy through robins, dandelions and other things that bring happy memories. He shares even more joy through His promises in the Bible. When we experience joy we experience a part of God.

Where is this found in the Bible?

For all the gods of the nations are idols, but the LORD made the heavens. Splendor and majesty are before him; strength and joy in his dwelling place (2 Chronicles 16:26-27).

"If you keep your feet from breaking the Sabbath and from doing as you please on my holy day, if you call the Sabbath a delight and the LORD's holy day honorable, and if you honor it by not going your own way and not doing as you please or speaking idle words, then you will find your joy in the LORD, and I will cause you to ride on the heights of the land and to feast on the inheritance of your father Jacob." The mouth of the LORD has spoken (Isaiah 58:13-14).

May the God of hope fill you with all joy and peace as you trust in him, so that you may overflow with hope by the power of the Holy Spirit (Romans 15:13).

But the fruit of the Spirit is love, joy, peace, patience, kindness, goodness, faithfulness, gentleness and self-control. Against such things there is no law (Galatians 5:22-23).

Read Nehemiah chapter 8:10

Summary

1. Joy dwells with God (2 Chronicles 16).
2. The joy of the Lord is your strength (Nehemiah 8).
3. Keeping God's law will enable us to find joy in the Lord (Isaiah 58).
4. Paul prays that God will fill the Roman Christians with joy in chapter 15.
5. The Holy Spirit produces joy (Galatians 5).

Why is this Important?

Very few people think of God as full of joy. We should treat God with respect. But God is also full of joy. When we properly relate to Him, we should also experience His joy.

I think happiness and joy are different. What is the difference? Many people seek happiness. They think happiness comes when everything goes well. No fighting, no sickness, plenty of money, lovely weather, no one telling them what to do, would all be part of this list to bring happiness. What would you add? Those things would sure bring me happiness but they might not bring joy.

God wants more. God wants us to experience joy. Joy can be experienced even when everything goes poorly. Happiness comes and goes but joy remains because it flows from the nature of God. Joy does not depend on happy conditions. Joy depends on your relationship to God.

People who find joy in God can even sing in prison. Read Acts 16:25. Paul and

Silas sang songs in prison because they were connected to God. They experienced the joy of God even though they were suffering.

When people experience God's joy they find unusual strength. Nehemiah says, "The joy of the Lord is your strength." Sometimes life can be very sad. People get sick. People suffer. People die. All of these things make us sad. When we put all our confidence in God, we find joy and strength even though we might be sad at the same time.

I'm glad God is joy. I want the Holy Spirit to fill my life with joy. Even if some things happen that make me sad, I want joy deep in my life at the same time. Joy helps me know I'm connected to God in the right way.

Something to Do:

- Ask three adults if they agree or disagree with the following statements: I can be happy only when I get what I want. The Holy Spirit can fill me with joy even when I do not get what I want. If they agree, ask them why. If they disagree, ask them why.

Something to Think About:

- When parents name a child "Joy" what are they hoping?
- Having joy when life is bad is something like knowing that a sad movie has a happy ending. If that is true, what kind of an ending should life have?
- Jesus wants his followers to show this joy to the world. Would you like God's joy to fill your life? Have you told Him?

17. God is Kind

Today was our third day in wilderness camp. Larry had not eaten very much the first two days. Larry's mother was an excellent cook but she didn't come to camp. Larry's friends had cooked the first two days. Maybe that was why he hadn't eaten very much. Today, Larry had to cook. He had been cooking today's meal for a long time. All the boys were getting hungry.

Soon the meal was ready. The boys offered thanks to God and everybody took their share. Larry didn't take much as usual. He was waiting for dessert. He loved banana pudding and he had fixed a whole pot full for dessert.

Larry eagerly watched each boy finish his meal. He knew what was next. Slowly, carefully, he measured each serving. One cup full went to each boy. As Larry finally filled his cup a big smile came across his face.

With his cup and spoon, Larry started to sit down on a big rock. Just then, the most horrible thing happened. Larry lost his balance, fell off the rock, and spilled all his banana pudding. Big tears filled his eyes.

I watched all this happen from a short distance away. I felt so sorry that big tears started to come to my eyes. Then, the most wonderful thing happened.

Larry now sat on the rock with his empty cup. Each boy got up, walked by, and spooned some pudding into Larry's cup.

Wow, those boys were kind.

God is like that. God is kind. He cares when we hurt. He hurts when our sin causes us pain. He wants to comfort us when we are sad. God is kind.

Where is this found in the Bible?

So God was kind to the midwives and the people increased and became even more numerous. And because the midwives feared God, he gave them families of their own (Exodus 1:20-21).

Then the angel of the LORD said, "LORD Almighty, how long will you withhold mercy from Jerusalem and from the towns of Judah, which you have been angry with these seventy years?" So the LORD spoke kind and comforting words to the angel who talked with me (Zechariah 1:12-13).

"May the LORD be with you as he has been with my father. [14] But show me unfailing kindness like that of the LORD as long as I live, so that I may not be killed, [15] and do not ever cut off your kindness from my family—not even when the LORD has cut off every one of David's enemies from the face of the earth" (1 Samuel 20:14-15).

"But let him who boasts boast about this: that he understands and knows me, that I am the LORD, who exercises kindness, justice and righteousness on earth, for in these I delight," declares the LORD (Jeremiah 9:24).

But when the kindness and love of God our Savior appeared, he saved us, not because of righteous things we had done, but because of his mercy. He saved us through the washing of rebirth and renewal by the Holy Spirit, whom he poured out on us generously through Jesus Christ our Savior (Titus 3:4-6).

Read Luke 6:32-35, Romans 2:1-4 and 1 Corinthians 13:4-5

Summary:

1. God was kind to the women who helped mothers have their babies (Exodus 1).
2. God spoke kind words to an angel who questioned him (Zechariah 1).
3. God is kind to ungrateful and wicked people (Luke 6).
4. Love is kind and God is love (I Corinthians 13 and I John).
5. If we say we know God, we must say that He is a God who shows kindness (Jeremiah 9).
6. God's kindness leads us to repentance (Romans 2).
7. God's kindness appeared as Jesus our savior (Titus 3).

Why is this Important?

The Bible teaches that God is bigger and stronger than anybody or anything. We know that God must be respected, feared, worshiped and obeyed. When I think about His size and power I just want to stay out of God's way. At times like that I need to remember that God is also kind.

We may wonder how God will speak with us when we question Him. We may wonder if God cares about us when we do so little for Him. We may wonder how God will treat us if we have been ungrateful or wicked. If we wonder about any of those things, we can read again and again how kind God treated people in the Bible. We know that He treats everyone the same. We can expect Him to be kind to us even though we may not deserve it.

A young Albanian teenager was given a New Testament. She did not know anything about God. But she began to read the Gospels. She told me, "I fell in love with Jesus because He was so kind to the people." She became a Christian and now works among the children of Albania telling them about the kind Jesus she came to love. Jesus is God's best expression of kindness.

God wants to be known for his kindness. He wants kindness to be part of his reputation among the people of the world. Because God is big and powerful and kind, I want to be near Him. When I read how kind He is to people, I'm like the girl from Albania and I too fall more in love with God.

Something to Do:

Interview five people in your home and/or neighborhood. Ask them about the kindest thing anyone ever did for them. Record their answers on an MP3 video recorder or even an old cassete player. Were all the answers different or were some the same? Did any of them mention God? Of all the answers you heard, which was the "kindest"?

Something to Think About:

- In your opinion, what was the kindest thing God ever did? Why do you think that?
- Do you think Christians are kind like God tells them to be?
- If you could be kind to the meanest person you know, who would that be and what would you do?
- What do you think would happen to you if God were not kind to you?

18. God is Life

I sat on his bed and watched him struggle to breathe. My father was eighty-five years old. He was born in 1903 and saw the world change a lot in his lifetime. Here are a few things invented during his life:

- Airplanes
- Personal computers
- Space travel.
- Fax machines
- Telephone
- Penicillin
- Television

Many of the things that we take for granted today were new and exciting when my father was a little boy. Radios, cars and electric lights were luxuries for some people. The doctor said he might live a few hours or days but he would surely die. I thanked God he was not in any pain. I planned to stay the night with him in his room. The nurse gave him a cool bath to bring down his fever. The nurse said I should go home since my Dad seemed to feel better. He looked so peaceful. I agreed. I knew I could not sleep but perhaps I could rest a little.

I got home very late. Just after I closed my eyes the phone rang. My father had died. Life slipped away. I was sorry I had gone home. I was glad I had told him how much I loved him many times. I asked the nurse on the phone to leave him alone until I returned. I wanted to see him one more time before they took him to the funeral home.

Life is the greatest mystery of all. No one really understands it or can precisely define it. When people die, we say, "Life is gone." But we don't really know why life goes away. The answer lies in the nature of God Himself. God created all kinds of life because He is life. He gives life and takes it away as He chooses. Everything depends on God for life. Without God, nothing has life. God is life. That night God took my father's life. One day, He will take my life.

Where is this found in the Bible?

In the sight of God, who gives life to everything, and of Christ Jesus, who while testifying before Pontius Pilate made the good confession, I charge you to keep this command without spot or blame until the appearing of our Lord Jesus Christ (1 Timothy 6:13-14).

We know that we are children of God, and that the whole world is under the control of the evil one. We know also that the Son of God has come and has given us understanding, so that we may know him who is true. And we are in him who is true—even in his Son Jesus Christ. He is the true God and eternal life (I John 5:19-20).

This day I call heaven and earth as witnesses against you that I have set before you life and death, blessings and curses. Now choose life, so that you and your children may live and that you may love the LORD your God, listen to his voice, and hold fast to him. For the LORD is your life, and he will give you many years in the land he swore to give to your fathers, Abraham, Isaac and Jacob (Deuteronomy 30:19-20).

"Blessed be your glorious name, and may it be exalted above all blessing and praise. You alone are the LORD. You made the heavens, even the highest heavens, and all their starry host, the earth and all that is on it, the seas and all that is in them. You give life to everything, and the multitudes of heaven worship you (Nehemiah 9:5-6).

In his hand is the life of every creature and the breath of all mankind (Job 12:10).

Through him all things were made; without him nothing was made that has been made. In him was life, and that life was the light of men (John 1:3-4).

Read John chapters 1, 3 and 5

Summary:

1. God is eternal life (I John 5).
2. God declares He is the life of Israel (Deuteronomy 30).
3. God gives life to everything (Nehemiah 9).

4. God sustains the life of every man and every creature (Job 12).
5. Life cannot exist outside of God (John 1).
6. Those who believe Jesus did die for their sin have eternal life (John 3).
7. God gives life back to those who have died physically (John 5).

Why is this Important?

I just got back from the toy store. You know what I found there? I found a doll that looked exactly like a human baby. She had eyes that opened and shut. Her hair was long and curly. She could drink a bottle of water, speak a few words, and even make her diaper wet. She also cost a lot of money.

That doll hardly compares to my granddaughter. In five years, the doll will look exactly the same, but Meridee will have changed in amazing ways. So what is the difference? Life! Meridee is alive. The earth is full of living things.

We call all of this natural life. Natural life is imperfect. Everything with natural life dies.

The Bible speaks of something different than natural life. The Bible uses words like new life, eternal life, and abundant life to describe life different from natural life. The Bible describes this kind of life as spiritual life. Spiritual life is as different from natural human life as a doll is from a human baby. Everyone knows that natural life begins at birth. Jesus taught that spiritual life begins at new birth.

God gives both natural life and spiritual life. Everything and everyone receives natural life from God because God is life.

No one chooses to be born naturally. Everyone must choose if they want to be born spiritually. You are born spiritually when you believe that Jesus died for your sin. Do you believe that? If you do, the Bible declares that you have spiritual life and spiritual life is eternal life. Congratulations for making the most important decision of your life.

Jesus said, “I am the way, the truth, and the life. No one comes unto the Father except by me” (John 14:6) God is life and the way to eternal life is believing Jesus died for your sin.

Something to Do:

- If there is a doctor in your church or if your parents have a friend who is a doctor ask them what tests they use to determine when life leaves a person or death occurs.

- Go to a library and look up a book about vets. Does it tell you what happens when an animal dies?
- Count the number of living things in your home. (Hint: plants are living too.)
- Plant a seed in a cup. How does the root know to go down and the stem go up? Are you amazed at a God who can put that information and more in each and every seed?

Something to Think About:

- In what ways does the life in plants and animals differ?
- Why do you think we get sad when a pet dies but not when a plant dies?
- God gives natural life to everyone but requires people to choose between eternal life or eternal death. Those who believe that Jesus has paid for their sin have chosen eternal life. Those who don't have chosen death. Why would someone not choose eternal life?
- Have you decided whether or not you believe Jesus paid for your sin when He died?
- If those who believe receive eternal life, what is eternal death like? Look in Matthew 25:41.

19. God is Light

One beautiful afternoon my friends and I hiked into a small valley to play. As the sun began to set, someone asked if we should hike the path out of the valley. I had excellent night vision at the time. So I assured everyone darkness would not be a problem. I would lead the group up the path after dark. I did not anticipate what giant redwoods do at night.

As a child I heard my parents say, “It’s so dark you cannot see your hand in front of your face.” That night I understood what they meant. The giant redwood trees block the sun during the day and block all light from the moon and stars at night. We literally could not see our hands when we held them up to our faces.

Since we hiked down during the day, no one thought to bring a flashlight. I had never experienced anything so dark. No light from the city. No moon. No stars. We felt like we were dipped in a vat of chocolate. I began to worry. How would we get up the path? Our choices were simple. We could stay in the valley until morning, or we could crawl up the path. We crawled on our hands and knees all the way out of that valley. My friends were not impressed with my night vision!

I learned a lot about darkness that night. I also learned that night vision needs a light from some source. Today I keep flashlights everywhere. You’ll even find one in my briefcase. I don’t want to ever have to crawl again.

The Bible says God is light. He is the source of both physical light and spiritual light. Without God, we are simply crawling around in the dark.

Where is this found in the Bible?

Many are asking, "Who can show us any good?" Let the light of your face shine upon us, O LORD (Psalm 4:6).

He wraps himself in light as with a garment; He stretches out the heavens like a tent (Psalm 104:2).

I saw that from what appeared to be his waist up he looked like glowing metal, as if full of fire, and that from there down he looked like fire; and brilliant light surrounded him. Like the appearance of a rainbow in the clouds on a rainy day, so was the radiance around him. This was the appearance of the likeness of the glory of the LORD. When I saw it, I fell facedown (Ezekiel 1:27-28).

Do not gloat over me, my enemy! Though I have fallen, I will rise. Though I sit in darkness, the LORD will be my light (Micah 7:8).

This is the message we have heard from him and declare to you: God is light; in him there is no darkness at all (I John 1:5).

Read Psalm 27:1

Summary:

1. The face of God is light (Psalm 4).
2. David says God is his light (Psalm 27).
3. The Psalmist describes God as wrapped in light (Psalm 104).
4. Ezekiel describes the glory of God which surrounds Him as brilliant light.
5. Micah says God is his light (Micah 7).
6. John says God is light (1 John 1).

Why is this Important?

The writers of the Bible help us understand more about God when they tell us He is light. He is the creator and sustainer of physical light but He is more than the sun and the stars.

We know that light is essential to our world. Plants must have light to grow. Without plants, most animals have nothing to eat. Without plants or animals, we have nothing to eat. Our world cannot survive without light. One day God's light will replace the sun so there will be no night.

God lights up every kind of darkness. He is physical light, and spiritual light.

He is every kind of light. The Bible also describes a kind of moral and spiritual darkness. Everything is easily seen in the presence of God. That means ordinary people do not see life from God's point of view unless they listen to God. Many people prefer their own point of view. They do not consider what God says. They remain in moral and spiritual darkness. Those who listen and do what He says walk in spiritual light.

People need both physical light and spiritual light to please God. People who do evil things live in spiritual darkness. They do not see the path that leads to eternal life. They will remain in spiritual darkness until they believe what God says in the Bible. Those who listen to God and do what He says walk in spiritual light. They know which good things to do. They know which evil things to avoid. They grow stronger every day in the spiritual light just like plants grow stronger in the physical light.

Something to Do:

- Turn off the lights. Have a parent light a candle. What is the difference between light and dark? What is the safest? Is it better to be in the light or the dark when you are in danger?
- Draw a picture of a lighthouse. How does that light save people?
- The light that God offers shows us how to get eternal life. Write the words 'Jesus is the Light of the World' in as many bright colors as possible.

Something to Think About:

- Have you ever wondered what God would look like if you could see Him?
- Why do you think Ezekiel fell face down when He saw the brilliant light? Have you ever been that scared?
- The Bible says the Devil disguises himself as an "angel of light" (2 Corinthians 11:14). Why do you think He chooses that disguise? In what ways do you think he tries to imitate God?

20. God is Love

The day sparkled and the crisp air made David and I glad to be outside. David had a young bird dog named Mischief that he wanted to train. The dog would live up to his name before the day was over.

We decided to walk through a large piece of land and let the dog get accustomed to the smells of the field. This young bird dog had lived his whole life in a pen and played only in David's back yard. Now he had to learn lessons from the great outdoors.

Meadowlarks flew ahead of us as the dog leaped through the grass. We joked and talked as we watched the dog go over a small hill out of sight. We knew he wouldn't go far. As we topped the hill ourselves, we stopped dead in our tracks. We could hardly believe our eyes. What we saw next will live in my memory forever.

Mischief met a skunk! Mischief had never seen a skunk so he barked playfully. The little skunk pointed his business end in Mischief's face and sprayed him unmercifully. I never felt so sorry for a dog in my life. He got so sick.

What Mischief did with the smell seems funny now, but it didn't seem funny then. Dogs are pack animals. They live together, hunt together, and sleep together. They don't like to be alone and howl when lonely. Domestic dogs love their humans as if they belonged to the pack. So, for Mischief, David and I were his pack...especially David!

Poor Mischief was so disoriented by the skunk's spray. Instinct drove him to "return to the pack" and that meant David. The dog wanted to get as close to David as possible. That was the last thing David wanted. He tried everything to make Mischief go away. Nothing worked.

Boy did that dog smell bad! David didn't smell that great either. Pretty soon all Mischief wanted to do was rub on David.

When I think about God's love for us, we're very like Mischief. We stink from sin inside and out. Sin has made us sick and disgusting. We need to be close to God. Unlike David, God wants to gather us up, stink and all and pull us close to Himself. That's love! I can't understand why Jesus would love sinners who don't love Him and save them from sin as well! But He does! He loves because God is love!

Where is that found in the Bible?

Give thanks to the LORD, for he is good. His love endures forever (Psalm 136:1).

For God so loved the world that he gave his one and only Son, that whoever believes in him shall not perish but have eternal life (John 3:16).

For I am convinced that neither death nor life, neither angels nor demons, neither the present nor the future, nor any powers, neither height nor depth, nor anything else in all creation, will be able to separate us from the love of God that is in Christ Jesus our Lord (Romans 8:38-39).

Aim for perfection, listen to my appeal, be of one mind, live in peace. And the God of love and peace will be with you (2 Corinthians 13:11).

Whoever does not love does not know God, because God is love (1 John 4:8).

Read Exodus 34

Why is this Important?

Many people use the word "love" to describe God. Unfortunately, it's the most popular word to describe many things. For example, we say, I love my Mom, I love my bicycle, and I love my dog.

Why do we use the same word to describe our Mom, our bicycle and our dog? Obviously we don't "love" them in the same way. When I say, "I love something", most of the time I mean, "It makes me happy." I wish English had a bigger and better word to use with God.

In the story you just read, God was not like my friend David. God does not push us away. He wants to pull us close to Himself. Amazingly, God offers to clean off the stink too! When God finishes with us, we will be fresh and new and perfect - without any sin to spoil us.

Some religions have gods who judge them. Some have gods who are everywhere. Only the God of the Bible loves us while we stink and offers to clean us up. Without God, we would live in our stink forever. That is what hell will be like. Hell will be full of people who chose to live in their own stink. I'm glad God is love.

When the Bible says, "God is love," it means God is the source of all love. All love begins with God. Love describes part of His basic nature. God loves people because He is love, He doesn't have to try. God wants us to love like He loves. When anyone loves anything, they show everyone what God is like in a small way.

Something to Do:

• When it's time to empty your kitchen bin have a look at what's inside. Does it look nice? Does it smell nice? Imagine what it would be like if you rubbed that rubbish all over you. Imagine what it would be like if you smelled like that all day every day. God loves us even when we are as horrible as that. Sin is even more offensive to God than stinky smells are to us.

Something to Think About:

• What do you say to someone who says to you, "I love you!"? What will you say to God who says He loves you?

• What do you suppose God wants us to do in response to His love?

• The Bible defines love as being "patient" and "kind". Why do you think these are so hard to be?

• Why do you think God has to command us to be "patient" and "kind"?

21. God is Merciful

My father owned his own business. A man who worked for him stole a lot of money from the business. When my dad found out, he fired him. The man had already spent the money, so he could not repay what he had stolen.

Not long after that, the man became sick. He had to stay in a hospital for several months. His family struggled because the man could not work. One day, my dad asked me if I wanted to go with him to visit this man and his family. I always wanted to go with my dad. In the car, he told me the story about this man.

I was very angry. I asked my dad if we were going to put that man in prison for what he had done. My dad said simply, "No." When I asked, "Why?", he replied, "I like to sleep at night." I wondered what he meant.

I did not understand. Why were we going to visit this family? Why shouldn't we make the man pay back the money or send him to prison?

We drove up to the man's house. His wife was in the front yard watching the children play. I became pretty nervous. I thought this family would hate us.

Then my dad did something that I will never forget. He got out of the car and gave the lady some money! Her husband appeared at the door and he and his wife had tears in their eyes. That man deserved to go to prison but my dad was merciful. He cared about the man and his family. He gave them what they did not deserve, more money. God is like that. He gives people what they do not deserve. He forgives their sins if they just believe that Jesus' death paid for their sin.

Where is this found in the Bible?

For the LORD your God is a merciful God; he will not abandon or destroy you or forget the covenant with your forefathers, which he confirmed to them by oath (Deuteronomy 4:31).

For many years you were patient with them. By your Spirit you admonished them through your prophets. Yet they paid no attention, so you handed them over to the neighboring peoples. But in your great mercy you did not put an end to them or abandon them, for you are a gracious and merciful God (Nehemiah 9:30-31).

Be merciful, just as your Father is merciful (Luke 6:36).

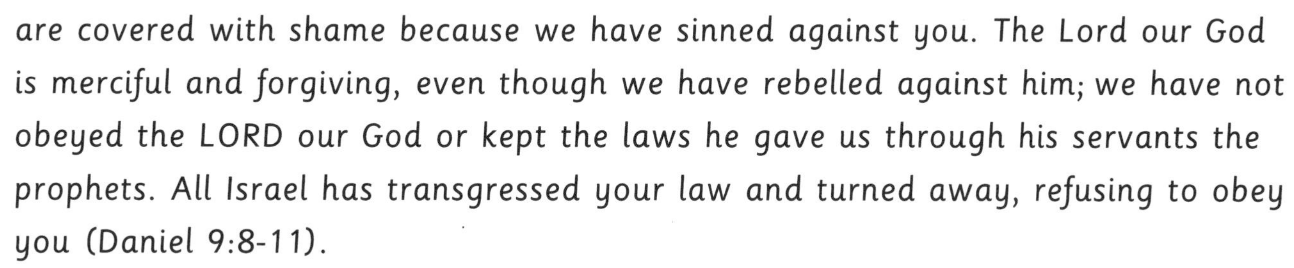

O LORD, we and our kings, our princes and our fathers are covered with shame because we have sinned against you. The Lord our God is merciful and forgiving, even though we have rebelled against him; we have not obeyed the LORD our God or kept the laws he gave us through his servants the prophets. All Israel has transgressed your law and turned away, refusing to obey you (Daniel 9:8-11).

Read Jeremiah 3:12

Summary:

1. Moses tells us that God is merciful (Deuteronomy 4).
2. God calls Israel to return to Him because He is merciful (Jeremiah 3).
3. Daniel confesses the sin of his people to the merciful God (Daniel 9).
4. Nehemiah reviews how merciful God was with Israel (Nehemiah 9).
5. Jesus declares our heavenly Father is merciful (Luke 6).

Why is this Important?

In the story the man clearly stole money from my dad. He was in real trouble. No one questioned that. He was guilty. He deserved punishment. He needed mercy.

What could the man do? He couldn't say to my dad, "Yes, I know I stole a lot of money, but could you give me some more?" What if that man stubbornly refused to accept my dad's offer? In either case we would say that man was crazy. But people do crazy things all the time. That is why they get in trouble. When they get in trouble, they need mercy.

The Bible says every one is in trouble with God. In fact, we were born in trouble. Adam and Eve created so much trouble for us that there is nothing we can do to make it right. If God did not come to us with an offer of mercy, we would stay in trouble forever separated from God. We need mercy from God.

God is full of mercy. He comes to us just like my dad did to that man. God offers us His mercy in the person of Jesus Christ. Jesus takes care of our trouble with God because he died on the cross to pay for our sin. That's God's mercy. If we don't accept God's offer of mercy, we're just as crazy as that man would have been if he had refused to accept money from my dad.

I'm so glad God is merciful. I know I can go to Him no matter how much trouble I'm in. I love Him for being merciful.

Something to Do:

- Draw a picture of a time someone was merciful to you. Put a happy face on the picture if you remembered to say "thank you".
- See if you can find a way to show mercy to someone at school this week.

Something to Think About:

- Can you think of reasons why you need God's mercy?
- Have you accepted God's offer of mercy?
- Can you think of a time last week when you could have been merciful? Were you? Was it hard or easy?
- What do you think would cause you to want to be more merciful?
- Is it easier to be merciful to your family or your friends? Why?
- Is it possible to show different amounts of mercy?
- How do you thank God for being merciful to you?

22. God is Musical

One, two, three! One, two, three! My piano teacher tapped out the rhythm of the song. As she counted, I was supposed to play the right keys on the piano. I could hear the tune in my head. My short stubby fingers simply refused to hit the right keys.

"Stop!" the teacher said. "Listen to how the song should be played". I always liked listening to my teacher play. Her long slender fingers would glide over the keys and wonderful music rose off the keyboard.

Now it was my turn again. Why did piano lessons have to come after a long day in school? My little fingers stumbled over the keys again and again. I thought the lesson would never end.

My mother insisted I take piano lessons. She applauded every pitiful attempt I made. I practiced the simple tunes over and over again. My teacher agonized over my lack of improvement. I never mastered the piano.

I still love music. Violins, trumpets, pianos and saxophones are all my favorites. Harps, flutes and ten string guitars are in there too. I would find it difficult to name an instrument I did not like. I especially like them together in a big band or orchestra.

I've heard music made by God. On warm spring days birds fill the woods with wonderful sounds. Chirps, warbles and peeps combine to make an outdoor symphony. Each little bird challenges your ear to hear his song. In only a matter of minutes, I can pick out twenty or twenty-five different tunes. Who taught them? God did! God loves music. God is musical.

Where is this found in the Bible?

The priests took their positions, as did the Levites with the LORD's musical instruments, which King David had made for praising the LORD and which were used when he gave thanks, saying, "His love endures forever." Opposite the Levites, the priests blew their trumpets, and all the Israelites were standing (2 Chronicles 7:6).

The Israelites who were present in Jerusalem celebrated the Feast of Unleavened Bread for seven days with great rejoicing, while the Levites and priests sang to the LORD every day, accompanied by the LORD's instruments of praise (2 Chronicles 30:21).

Then the LORD will appear over them; his arrow will flash like lightning. The Sovereign LORD will sound the trumpet; he will march in the storms of the south (Zechariah 9:14).

On the Lord's Day I was in the Spirit, and I heard behind me a loud voice like a trumpet, which said: "Write on a scroll what you see and send it to the seven churches: to Ephesus, Smyrna, Pergamum, Thyatira, Sardis, Philadelphia and Laodicea" (Revelation 1:10-11).

After this I looked, and there before me was a door standing open in heaven. And the voice I had first heard speaking to me like a trumpet said, "Come up here, and I will show you what must take place after this" (Revelation 4:1).

Read I Thessalonians 4:16

Summary:

1. Musical instruments in the temple belonged to the Lord (2 Chronicles 7 and 30).
2. Zechariah tells us that the Lord will sound a trumpet on the Day of Judgment.
3. Christians will be raised from the dead when God sounds the trumpet (1 Thessalonians 4).
4. The voice of God sounded like a trumpet (Revelation 1 and 4).

Why is this Important?

Sometimes we forget that God is musical. Or we think He likes only one kind of music...organ music! We must remember that God invented all kinds of music. Music touches us deep inside. Happy music makes us want to tap our feet. Sad music helps us grieve. College bands and armies march to music. Symphonies play music that tells a story.

In 2 Chronicles there is a variety of musical instruments. God wanted the Levites to play them in the temple. From other passages we know they used tambourines, cymbals, harps and flutes and many more. The writer calls these the Lord's instruments of praise. What a wonderful way to use music. We sing in church to give God the music of our soul.

God devoted a whole book in the Bible to music. The book of Psalms is a book of songs. The Psalms offer prayers, tell stories, express sadness, thanksgiving, praise and joy. The book of Psalms may be the most popular book in the entire Bible. God uses that book to help us remember His great promises and truth about His character. When you read the Psalms, you will notice the words are there but the music is missing. God lets you make up any tune you wish.

God must be musical. Who else could teach birds to sing and angels to play trumpets? When I'm listening to one of my favorite pieces of music, I'm remembering God invented music. God is musical.

Something to Do:

- Find as many musical "things" as you can around the house and put them in one place. Can you play "Jesus Loves Me" on one or more of these instruments. You may need more than one instrument to make all the notes.
- Make a list or take a picture of everything you can use to make music.
- Try to write a new song or tune with a simple melody using 6-8 notes.

Something to Think About:

- Can you play a musical instrument?
- If not, which one would you like to play? Are you willing to work hard at practicing?
- What is your favorite song? Do you know why you like it? Melody? Rhythm? Instrument? Performer?
- When God sings, what do you suppose it sounds like?
- Would you like to sing or hum a song to God? Do you think God would enjoy your song even if it is not perfect?
- Do you think God smiles when we sing to Him at church?
- Listen to *The Little Drummer Boy* song. When you sing do you offer up your songs to God the same way he did? Would you like to?

23. God is Mysterious

A slow drizzle made the chilly November day seem even colder. My Scoutmaster gave my four friends and me a small map and a compass. He let us out of the van and left us on a country road. His final words to us were, "Follow your map, and believe your compass. I'll have a pot of stew waiting when you get back to camp."

We were alone. No adults. Five boys with a map and compass. We had to find our way back to the camp.

The drizzle blurred our vision. We could not see far. The clouds blocked our view of the sun. We twisted and turned the map trying to make it agree with the compass. Our compass contained a tiny magnetized steel needle. The needle always pointed north unless we placed the compass too close to metal or a magnet. The compass worked because the north and south poles of the earth act like a giant magnet.

We began our hike. Everything went well until half the group decided the compass was not working. They decided to find their way without the compass. My half followed the compass and got back to camp about two hours before the other half. That cold drizzly day brightened up when we got our first bowl of stew.

We don't know exactly why magnets work. Magnets are mysterious. We don't really understand why the earth works like a magnet. The earth's magnetic field is mysterious.

God is like that. We don't understand everything about Him. God is mysterious. But we must trust Him if we are to find our way.

Where do we find that in the Bible?

Can you fathom the mysteries of God? Can you probe the limits of the Almighty? They are higher than the heavens—what can you do? They are deeper than the depths of the grave—what can you know? (Job 11:7-8).

But in the days when the seventh angel is about to sound his trumpet, the mystery of God will be accomplished, just as he announced to his servants the prophets (Revelation 10:7).

The secret things belong to the LORD our God, but the things revealed belong to us and to our children forever, that we may follow all the words of this law (Deuteronomy 29:29).

As it is written: "No eye has seen, no ear has heard, no mind has conceived what God has prepared for those who love him" (1 Corinthians 2:9).

Read Colossians 2:2

Summary:

1. Job asks who can understand the mysteries of God? Job did not expect an answer because no one can understand them (Job 11).
2. Paul explains that one mystery of God was revealed when Jesus Christ came to the earth (Colossians 2).
3. John tells us that another mystery of God will be finished when the angel blows the 7th trumpet of judgment (Revelation 10).
4. Moses tells us that secret things belong to God alone (Deuteronomy 29).
5. God has prepared a final mystery for those who love Him (1 Corinthians 2).

Why is this Important?

Some mysteries about God have been revealed. One great mystery from the Old Testament involved how God would permanently deal with sin. We knew He intended to send a savior. How he would do it was a great mystery - and then Jesus, God's only Son, came to die for His people.

Some mysteries about God are still in the future. God's judgment on the world is still a mystery. We know it is certain. We don't know when it will happen. God's plan for those who love Him is also still a mystery. God has something so wonderful prepared that no human could ever imagine how good it will be. That is quite a promise. I can imagine some amazing things. God says, "My plan is even better!"

Many things about God remain a mystery. In the story you just read, we didn't understand the earth's magnetic field. My group trusted the compass to find the camp.

We trust God even though we don't understand everything about Him. We need Him to find our way in life. Even if we could remember everything the Bible says about God, we would still have to admit, "God is mysterious."

Something to Do:

• Find a refrigerator magnet and some small nails. Connect one nail to the magnet. This will cause the nail to be temporarily magnetized so as long as it is stuck to the magnet it will cause other small nails to stick to itself. Do you have to understand everything about magnets to use them to stick things to the refrigerator? Would you need to understand everything about God to trust Him? If you believe the Bible, we know more about God than we do about refrigerator magnets.

Something to Think About:

• Does it bother you when you cannot explain everything about God?

• What is the most (important) mysterious thing you wish you could explain about God?

• Why do you think people want to explain everything about God?

• Are there things about yourself you cannot explain? What are they? Are you a little mysterious in some ways?

24. God is Patient

Our daughter was so small. She could pull herself up on the furniture, but she could not walk by herself. Her mother and I spent a lot of time on the floor with her.

One night, I helped her stand to her feet. Her mother held out her arms. "Come to Mommy, walk to Mommy!" Kimberly got so excited. She quickly forgot to hold on to something. She took several small steps all by herself before she fell into her mother's arms. We both cheered so loud, you would think she had won an Olympic medal.

Now her mother helped her stand. I held out my arms. "Come to Daddy, walk to

Daddy!" Back and forth she went. That night marked the beginning of her learning to walk.

Her mother and I worked with her every day. But it took a lot of practice. Each time she fell, one of us would pick her up. We praised her and encouraged her to start again. We never got tired of helping and she never got tired of trying.

Today our daughter walks by herself. I suppose if she were still trying to learn how to walk, we would still try to help her. That would require a lot more patience.

God is like that. He is patient with us. He wants to teach us how to live correctly. He is a lot more patient with us than we were with our daughter. God must be patient with us all our lives. I am glad he is patient with me.

Where is this found in the Bible?

The Lord is not slow in keeping his promise, as some understand slowness. He is patient with you, not wanting anyone to perish, but everyone to come to repentance (2 Peter 3:9).

And he passed in front of Moses, proclaiming, "The LORD, the LORD, the compassionate and gracious God, slow to anger, abounding in love and faithfulness, maintaining love to thousands, and forgiving wickedness, rebellion and sin. Yet he does not leave the guilty unpunished; he punishes the children and their children for the sin of the fathers to the third and fourth generation" (Exodus 34:6-7).

But you, O Lord, are a compassionate and gracious God, slow to anger, abounding in love and faithfulness (Psalm 86:15).

'The LORD is slow to anger, abounding in love and forgiving sin and rebellion. Yet he does not leave the guilty unpunished; he punishes the children for the sin of the fathers to the third and fourth generation' (Numbers 14:18).

But the fruit of the Spirit is love, joy, peace, patience, kindness, goodness, faithfulness, gentleness and self-control. Against such things there is no law (Galatians 5:22-23).

Summary:

1. Peter explains why God appears to work so slowly. He is patient (2 Peter 3).
2. In the book of Exodus God describes His own character to Moses. Among His qualities, He lists, "...slow to anger...". These words are also mentioned in the book of Psalms and the book of Numbers (Exodus 34; Psalm 86; Numbers 14).
3. Paul says the Holy Spirit reproduces God's character in the life of the Christian. Patience is specifically mentioned among other qualities of God (Galatians 5).

Why is this Important?

In the story you just read, we were patient with our baby girl because she was little and wanted to learn. Would we have been as patient if she had not tried so hard? I don't know. What if she had not tried at all? What if every time we held her up she cried and refused to stand? I think I would have become more and more impatient.

Patience means not getting angry or frustrated. When I become impatient I get angry more quickly. I'm glad God does not get angry with me as quickly as I do with others. The Old Testament tells us how slowly God gets angry. God is patient. Each time we fail, if we are a child or an adult, God patiently picks us up and helps us start fresh. Sometimes I wonder if God gets tired of my failure. When I do, I remember the wonderful words, "God is slow to anger; He is patient with you."

Not only do I need patience from God toward me, I need patience in my life to give to others. God works patiently with me and He also helps me be patient. When Paul mentions the fruit of the Spirit, he means God creates patience in me. I am certainly not as patient as I need to be. My wife will tell you I am a lot more patient than I used to be.

I'm really glad God is patient. I need lots of it and God has an unlimited supply. When I am patient I show how much God is working in me. When I am impatient, I show how little God is working in me.

Something to Do:

• Be a human remote control for the T.V. one evening. Change the channel on the T.V. but do not use the remote. (Before remote controls were invented everyone had to change channels by hand. Do you think people were more patient then? Why or why not?) Now think about the way God is patient with us all day every day. Do you love God more now that you think about his patience?

• Find the oldest video game you can. Why don't you enjoy playing with it? Why does it bore you?

Something to Think About:

• What things make you impatient or upset? Why?

• What things does God need to be patient with you about?

• If God were not patient with you, what would he do? What do you think he should do?

• When have you been angry quickly with people? Would you like to ask God to help you be slow to get angry the next time?

25. God is Playful

The sun slowly slipped toward the horizon on a lazy summer afternoon. My friend and I bobbed up and down in my boat. We fished quietly on our favorite lake. Suddenly a mother raccoon and her five small babies scrambled out of the bushes onto the shore just ahead. She did not see us. We kept so still we could almost hear ourselves breathe.

For fifteen minutes those babies entertained us. They had a wonderful time. They fell off logs. They shoved one another in the lake. They climbed over and under their mother. Raccoons cannot laugh and giggle like humans. If they could, those five babies would have created a lot of noise. Instead they fussed and hissed at each other as they splashed and played without a care in the world.

Mother, on the other hand, worked very hard to find dinner. She looked under every stone and stick hoping to find a crayfish or clam. Nothing those babies did interrupted her search. She went about as though those silly babies behaved perfectly normal. I wondered if mother raccoons ever scolded their babies. Finally they forced us to laugh out loud. Those babies were so playful and fun to watch.

Now, I'm sure most people do not think of God as playful. We think God is serious. And God is serious but could God have a playful side too? Who taught those babies to be so playful? The Bible tells us that creation reveals the character of God. God certainly is joyful and full of energy and life. Next time you enjoy playing ask God to be with you in your play. Thank Him for play and ask Him to help you to please Him and give Him joy.

Where is that found in the Bible?

The wolf will live with the lamb, the leopard will lie down with the goat, the calf and the lion and the yearling together; and a little child will lead them. The cow will feed with the bear, their young will lie down together, and the lion will eat straw like the ox. The infant will *play* near the hole of the cobra, and the young child put his hand into the viper's nest. They will neither harm nor destroy on all my holy mountain, for the earth will be full of the knowledge of the LORD as the waters cover the sea (Isaiah 11:6-9).

"This is what the Lord says: 'I will return to Zion and dwell in Jerusalem. Then Jerusalem will be called the City of Truth, and the mountain of the LORD Almighty will be called the Holy Mountain. This is what the LORD Almighty says: 'Once again men and women of ripe old age will sit in the streets of Jerusalem, each with cane in hand because of his age. The city streets will be filled with boys and girls playing there.' ... This is what the LORD Almighty says: 'The fasts of the fourth, fifth, seventh and tenth months will become joyful and glad occasions and happy festivals for Judah. Therefore love truth and peace.'" (Zechariah 8:3-5 and 19.)

Read Job 40:15-24.

Summary:

1. Isaiah describes a place and time where enemies and dangers will be different. A child will even play near the cobra's hole (Isaiah 11).
2. Job describes an animal some consider to be a dinosaur. Whatever he saw, there were many animals playing nearby. We know God created all the animals (Job 40).
3. Zechariah records the words of God who promises to rebuild Jerusalem and fill it with boys and girls who will play in the streets (Zechariah 8).
4. Zechariah also records God's promise to have happy parties full of joy in the 4th, 5th, 7th, and 10th month of every year!

Why is this Important?

Everyone knows we must treat God with respect. We also know that the world is full of serious problems. Famine, disease, floods, earthquakes and other natural disasters happen somewhere in the world every day. Humans make things worse through war, pollution, child abuse and terrorism to mention only a few.

Christians know how serious life really is. We know that the decisions we make about God and Jesus in this life will affect where we spend eternity. In the Bible, Hell is a very serious place. If we have made the right choice about Jesus Christ, we know that we will spend eternity with God. Now that is something to smile about.

Those who know they will live with God forever can really laugh. In fact, the Bible tells us to "rejoice". We know about life after death. We know one day all the problems we mentioned earlier will be gone.

Meanwhile, we need to appreciate the playful side of God. Play and fun remind us of that time in the future when laughter will be common. In that day, life will be more fun for everyone who loves God.

When you see baby animals playing or little children laughing, remember, God has a playful side. One day He plans for us to laugh and play and praise Him for being so wonderful and good and playful.

Something to Do:

- Find a video of real animals playing and think about God as you watch.
- Play with your family pet and think about God at the same time. (Try 10-15 minutes)
- Was it hard to play and think about God at the same time? Why or why not?
- Do you think God enjoyed watching you play as much as you did? Why? Why not?

Something to Think About:

- Do you think God smiles when animals or children play?
- Do you think God is looking forward to the time when those who love God can laugh and be joyful all the time?
- What do you think gives God joy? What pleases Him?

26. God is Righteous

Huffing and puffing, I finally reached the gate of the castle. I now knew why kings built castles on mountains. Enemies would have a difficult time hauling all their equipment up there. I had a difficult time hauling myself up! Gratefully, I was at the gate.

My friends and I bought our tickets and began our tour of the great castle. The kitchen was huge. You could roast a whole cow in the fire pit. Twenty-five loaves of bread would fit in the oven at one time. I did not see a microwave! I wondered who had to haul the firewood up the mountain everyday.

The king's rooms were high in the castle. From his windows you could see the whole countryside. No one could sneak up on you. I wondered what being king was like. I knew I didn't want to be a cook! But king! King sounded pretty good! I asked my friends if this castle had a king. They said, "no". I suggested that I should apply for the job, but they laughed at me.

I wondered what being king was really like. Kings did what they wanted. Sometimes they killed people who walked into their presence without being invited. Sometimes kings punished innocent people they did not like or forgave guilty people they did like! Kings made laws but didn't have to obey laws.

We believe that everyone should be treated fairly. We expect our courts to punish those who do wrong and protect those who do right. Kings did not always do those things.

God always does the right thing. God protects the innocent and punishes the guilty. He is righteous. That is why the Bible says He is King of kings. He is the best person you will ever meet. He always does what is right because He is completely good. There is nothing evil in God. Every good, fair and right thing begins in God.

Where is that found in the Bible?

"What has happened to us is a result of our evil deeds and our great guilt, and yet, our God, you have punished us less than our sins have deserved and have given us a remnant like this. Shall we again break your commands and intermarry with the peoples leaving us no remnant or survivor? O LORD, God of Israel, you are righteous! We are left this day as a remnant. Here we are before you in our guilt, though because of it not one of us can stand in your presence" (Ezra 9:13-15).

Can a mortal be more righteous than God? Can a man be more pure than his Maker? (Job 4:17).

O righteous God, who searches minds and hearts, bring to an end the violence of the wicked and make the righteous secure (Psalm 7:9).

The LORD is gracious and righteous; our God is full of compassion (Psalm 116:5)

Read Psalm 11:7 and Ecclesiastes 7:20

Summary:

1. God is declared righteous and Israel wicked (Ezra 9).
2. Job asks if a man can be as righteous as God. He expects a "No!" (Job 4).
3. Only a righteous God can deal effectively with wicked people (Psalm 7).
4. God loves justice (Psalm 11).
5. God is both righteous and gracious (Psalm 116).
6. Solomon tells us that no human is completely righteous (Ecclesiastes 7).

Why is this Important?

God is both King and Judge. Because He is righteous, He will be a good king and a fair judge. He makes good rules because He is good. He will judge every person who ever lived. He is always good, fair, and consistent. No one will escape from God. He will punish the wicked and reward those who trust Him.

Everyone who is punished by God will say God is right. Wicked people deserve to be punished. God offers to spare them if they believe Jesus was punished for them. If they refused Jesus' offer, they must pay for their own sin. They will receive their own punishment. God is righteous with the wicked.

God protects everyone who believes Jesus was punished for his or her sin. Jesus paid the full price. If anyone accepts Jesus' punishment, he does not have to be punished for his own sin. God is righteous with them because they accepted Jesus' punishment.

One day God will rule the earth as king and judge. He will fill it with His goodness, fairness and justice. Everything good begins with and comes from God. God is righteous. We will all be glad He is king.

Until then, I'm glad God is righteous. That gives me hope.

Something to Do:

• Would you like to play a game for a day? Here is the game. You must play the game from the time you get up until the time you go to bed. Pretend your mom or dad is King or Queen. If you did not ask permission to enter the room they are in EVERYTIME they might kill you! Ask permission every time you enter the room they are in. See if you can stay alive for a whole day. Are you glad our King is more patient with us? When you pray tonight, tell God how grateful you are. You can read about a real king like this in the Book of Esther in the Bible.

Something to Think About:

• Have you ever heard someone lie and not get caught or steal and not get caught? Do you think they will be surprised when God remembers exactly what they said and did? What will they say to God? Do you think He will believe them?

• How do you think people would act if they knew for sure they would always get caught and punished every time they lied or stole?

• It would be good not to do these things so we will not be embarrassed when God comes to take charge as king and judge. How will you remind yourself?

• How would the world be different if everyone did right all the time?

• Are you glad God plans to create a world just like that? If you are, tell Him tonight when you pray.

27. God is Strong

A summer storm brewed in the distance. I could smell it coming. In the summer, I always slept with my bed pushed next to the open window. That way I could smell the Gardenia bush outside. Tonight I smelled the storm. I could also hear the thunder rumble closer and closer.

This storm sounded like a bad one. I decided I did not want to be alone. I knew my Aunt Dodie would be awake. She always got up before the sun. I knocked quietly at her door. She invited me in. We watched out her window while we sat on her bed and listened to the thunder. I felt better.

Suddenly, a bolt of lightning hit the telephone pole in the back yard. The clap of thunder scared the "bejabbers" out of us. I've never seen anything so bright or heard anything so loud. I'll remember that bolt as long as I live.

Since then I've learned that one bolt of lightning can heat the air around it to 54,000°F. I cook chicken on the grill at 250°F. What would 54,000°F feel like? That is a massive amount of power.

In my life, I've survived flash floods, hurricanes, tornadoes and earthquakes. I've only seen volcanoes on TV and that is fine with me. While I was helpless against these powerful forces, God's power makes them all seem small – even that bolt of lightning. God has unlimited power. He can do whatever He wishes. No human being or group of human beings can stop God. God is really strong.

Word Fact: Another word for strong is Omnipotent. God is Omnipotent.

Where is this found in the Bible?

Who is this King of glory? The LORD strong and mighty, the LORD mighty in battle (Psalm 24:8).

One thing God has spoken, two things have I heard: that you, O God, are strong (Psalm 62:11).

Now may the Lord's strength be displayed, just as you have declared: (Numbers 14:17).

Ascribe to the LORD, O families of nations, ascribe to the LORD glory and strength (1 Chronicles 16:28).

Be exalted, O LORD, in your strength; we will sing and praise your might (Psalm 21:13).

Read Revelation 5: 11-12 and 1 Corinthians 1:23-24

Summary:

1. Innumerable angels sing to Jesus that He is worthy to receive all power from the Father (Revelation 5).
2. David tells us that the Lord is strong and mighty in Psalm 24.
3. Moses calls upon God to display His power in forgiving Israel in Numbers 14.
4. We are reminded to refer to God as strong (1 Chronicles 16).
5. David says we all should sing about the strength of God (Psalm 21).
6. Paul teaches that Jesus is the power of God (1 Corinthians 1).

Why is this Important?

In the story we talked about powerful forces in our world. Scientists call these, "forces of nature". Actually, God put these forces in place. They should be called the "forces of God". At the moment we cannot control these forces such as the wind, lightning, storms and earthquakes. They appear to be out of control. Sin has made creation behave in this scary, terrifying way.

These forces raise questions in our minds. Are we victims? Is anyone big enough to control them? Scientists study these forces and attempt to measure them and find out if humans can do anything to control them.

The world desperately needs God to control these forces, but many people refuse to admit God is the creator. If they admit that God created these powerful forces, they must also admit God created them. Many people do not want to admit God is their creator. Fortunately, the God who created the universe can also control it. God has unlimited strength and power.

When we say God is strong, we use a special word. We use a word which means God has no limits to his strength. We say, "God is omnipotent". That word can be sounded out like this, om-ni-po-tent. Say it several times and you will have a special word that describes God and impresses your friends.

Jesus showed the power of God again and again. Jesus persuaded the disciples that He could control the "forces of God" when He walked on the water and stilled the storm. (You can look these stories up for yourself in John 6:16-24 and Luke 8:22-25). He controlled them because He created them.

The Bible records many miracles. In each case, God simply shows His power over the forces He created. When people see miracles they often lose the proper focus. They are impressed by the miracle instead of loving the God of the miracle. God wants us to love Him more than the miracle or power to create the miracle.

Something to Do:

• People use lots of power in the world God created. Can you count all the things that need power in your home? For example, each light bulb needs power but a kitchen chair does not need power. Can you imagine how many things need power in all the homes in your neighborhood? Now remember, we have just learned how to use the power created by God. Now get a thimble and fill it with water. That thimble full of water is the amount of power used by humans. The water in the ocean might be like the power God really has.

Something to Think About:

• The next time some "force of God" happens close to you, what will you think about God?

• If God created human life, does He have the right to send any human to heaven or hell when He chooses?

• Read Romans 8:18-22: do you think some of the "groanings of creation" include earthquakes, tornadoes, hurricanes and volcanoes?

• God created the sun and stars and used up none of his power yet they are so powerful. What does this say about God's power?

28. God is Smart

In 1963, I asked Jesus Christ to be my savior. I believed that His death on the cross paid for my sin. I knew very little about the Bible. I wanted to learn everything in the Bible. I began to pray that God would give me an understanding of the Bible.

I thought God would teach me through a miracle. I hoped I would go to sleep one night and wake up the next morning knowing the Bible. God could do that but it never happened.

A few years later I found myself studying Hebrew, the language God used to write the Old Testament. My grades were poor and I complained to God. I felt He was letting me down. He reminded me about my prayer to know the Bible. He answered my prayer by allowing me to study it in the original language.

I had to really concentrate when I took my tests. If I didn't I could have forgotten something important. I worked hard to learn Hebrew. I was not the best student but I passed the course. Much of what I learned about Hebrew has slipped away from my memory. If I needed to remember those things, I would have to read my text books again. I know a lot more about the Bible than I did in 1963. I also know I will never learn everything there is to know in the Bible

God is not like me. He does not have to learn anything. He knows everything. He does not have to concentrate so He won't forget something. He knows everything all at once, and all the time. He knows what has happened and what will happen. He knows what could have happened and what has not happened. God is smart.

Word Fact: Another word for smart is Omniscient. God is Omniscient. He knows everything.

Where is that found in the Bible?

Who has understood the mind of the LORD, or instructed him as his counselor? (Isaiah 40:13).

However, as it is written: "No eye has seen, no ear has heard, no mind has conceived what God has prepared for those who love him" (1 Corinthians 2:9).

"Do not keep talking so proudly or let your mouth speak such arrogance, for the LORD is a God who knows, and by him deeds are weighed (1 Samuel 2:3).

If we had forgotten the name of our God or spread out our hands to a foreign god, would not God have discovered it, since he knows the secrets of the heart? (Psalm 44:20-21).

This then is how we know that we belong to the truth, and how we set our hearts at rest in his presence whenever our hearts condemn us. For God is greater than our hearts, and he knows everything (1 John 3:19-20).

Read Matthew 6:7-8 and Matthew 7:29-31

Summary:

1. No human has taught God anything (Isaiah 40).
2. Humans cannot imagine God's wonderful plan (1 Corinthians 2).
3. God knows when we brag about ourselves (1 Samuel 2).
4. God knows even the secrets of our heart (Psalm 44).
5. God knows what we need even before we ask Him (Matthew 6).
6. God knows everything (1 John 3).
7. God knows exactly how many hairs are on every head (Matthew 10).

Why is this Important?

Before 1546, in order to have even one book, you had to either have a lot of money or you had to make your own hand written copy. A long time ago before computers, television, or even electricity, every book had to be written by hand. Imagine making a hand written copy of just one of your schoolbooks. You would probably have to skip lunch and recess too! I'm glad I don't have to do that! I'm writing this chapter on August 15, 1998. 15,000 books will be published in the

United States today, and every day. I'm sure glad I don't have to copy them by hand. I could read every book published today in five years if I read a book every day. During those five years 27,375,000 more books would be published.

Imagine what it would be like to read and remember what was in all those books. I can't imagine how many books have been written throughout history. God does! He knows how many and He knows everything in those books. In fact, God knows what is in books that have not been written yet.

Here is the word we use to describe how smart God really is. We say, "God is omniscient". That simply means God knows everything.

God even knows what people think.

I'm glad God knows everything because that means no one will ever outsmart Him.

Something to Do:

- Go around your house and count all the books. Write down as many titles as you can in half an hour. How hard would you have to work to remember just the titles? Write down the number of pages in the longest book. Does it make your mind tired just to think about remembering everything in every book all at once and all the time?

Something to Think About:

- If you were going to write a book, what would you write about?
- You've been reading this book for a few days. Are there things you have already forgotten?
- Can you make a list of everything you remember "God is" so far?
- Are you surprised that God knows even the secret things about you?
- Can you find the only things God chooses not to remember? (Look in Hebrews 10:17)

29. God is Spirit

Have you ever seen a germ face to face? I haven't! My mother thought they were everywhere. Wash your hands before you eat! Brush your teeth before you go to bed! Take a bath! Wash, brush, bathe, or you will be covered with germs my mother insisted.

I didn't mind washing, too much, but what I hated the most was if I got a cut or scratch my mother would bathe it in iodine in order to kill those germs. It really stung! My mother never convinced me that the germs would hurt just as much as the iodine.

For most of history, humans have not known about germs. We had no way to see them. One day in the 17th century, Antoni van Leeuwenhoek invented the microscope. Now we see millions of living things too small for the natural eye. These living things have a different kind of life than we do.

God has a different kind of life than we do. God is spirit. We know He is alive the same way my mom knew those germs are alive. She could see that germs caused an infection. We see God's creation and know that He lives.

If Antoni had not invented the microscope, do you think my mother would still have swabbed those germs with iodine? Probably.

Where is this found in the Bible?

God is spirit, and his worshipers must worship in spirit and in truth (John 4:24).

You, however, are controlled not by the sinful nature but by the Spirit, if the Spirit of God lives in you. And if anyone does not have the Spirit of Christ, he does not belong to Christ (Romans 8:9).

Now the Lord is the Spirit, and where the Spirit of the Lord is, there is freedom (2 Corinthians 3:17).

Read Genesis 1:1 and 1 Corinthians 3:16

If you take your neighbor's cloak as a pledge, return it to him by sunset, because his cloak is the only covering he has for his body. What else will he sleep in? When he cries out to me, I will hear, for I am compassionate (Exodus 22:26-27).

Then the LORD came down in the cloud and stood there with him and proclaimed his name, the LORD. And he passed in front of Moses, proclaiming, "The LORD, the LORD, the compassionate and gracious God, slow to anger, abounding in love and faithfulness" (Exodus 34:5-6).

He prayed to the LORD, "O LORD, is this not what I said when I was still at home? That is why I was so quick to flee to Tarshish. I knew that you are a gracious and compassionate God, slow to anger and abounding in love, a God who relents from sending calamity" (Jonah 4:2).

Read 2 Chronicles 30:9

Summary:

1. God's willingness to forgive comes partly from his tenderhearted feelings for us (Ephesians 4).
2. God tells us to be compassionate because He is compassionate (Exodus 22).
3. God describes Himself to Moses as compassionate. (Exodus 34).
4. Jonah wishes God were not so compassionate (Jonah 4).
5. If Israel comes back to God after a time of discipline for sin then God will show compassion (2 Chronicles).

Why is this Important?

The Bible says God is big and powerful. When I think about His size and strength I wonder if I will be safe with Him. That is why I must remember that God is also tender in dealing with me. Not only does He say He's tender, He proves it by forgiving my sins.

In the Bible, God instructs those who love Him to care for the poor, the orphan, the widow and the prisoner. He asks us to represent Him. Every time we treat someone tenderly we show them a part of God.

In the story I called for my "mommy" because she tenderly cared for me. She also disciplined me when I disobeyed her. She corrected me when I said something wrong. God is both tender and a disciplinarian. That is what He wants to tell us.

If you need God to be tender with you, just ask Him. If you need discipline from God, just wait. He always disciplines His children.

God wants to be the first person we turn to when we're in trouble. Most of the time, we think of Him last. He wants to show us His tender care. I'm so glad he is tender. I need Him a lot.

Something to Do:

- Can you think of some things you might do to make your home a more tender place for your family?
- Ask your mother to explain how she treats a favorite house plant in a tender way.
- Ask a veterinarian how a pet can be treated in a tender way.
- Ask your mother and the vet what would happen if the plant or the animal were not treated in a tender way.
- Can you think of ways God has been tender with you like your mother is with the plant, or the vet is with the animal?

Something to Think About:

- Who is the most tender person you know?
- What exactly do they do that makes you feel they are tender?
- Does God do any of these same things?
- Do you feel better knowing that God really cares when you hurt?
- Has God ever used you to show His tenderness?

31. God is Timeless

Time for dinner; time to go to bed; time to get up; time to wash your hands. I never worried about time because mom would tell me when it was time to do something. Then I went to school and became personally interested in time. The only time during the day that I could control was lunch time. The rules were simple. You could play outside when you finished lunch until lunch time was over. I learned quickly that the faster you ate your lunch, the more time you had to play.

I took a very serious approach to lunchtime. Here was my plan.

1. Anticipate the lunch bell and get out of class quick.
2. Walk really fast to the lunchroom but don't run.
3. Gulp down my bag lunch.
4. Rush outside and play until the bell rang.

Do you like my plan? Each step in the plan required precise execution. Step 1 meant sitting as close to the door as possible and having your legs ready to take action as the bell rang. Step 2 had little margin for error. If you were caught running, lunchtime would be wasted in the principal's office! Step 3 depended on mom not packing something that required a lot of chewing. Step 4 required sunshine or no more than a light mist or we would have to stay inside.

My best time came with a sandwich cut in two, a banana, and three cookies. The sandwich took the longest time. You can almost get a small banana in your mouth at one time. Cookies went in the pocket for later. I clearly became the Olympic time champion of lunch!

As you can tell, I lived in a hurry at lunchtime. God is not like me at all. God does not act or live in a hurry. He is not controlled by time at all because He created time. God Himself is timeless.

Fact: Eternal is another word for Timeless. God is Eternal.

Where is this found in the Bible?

Lord, thou hast been our dwelling-place in all generations. Before the mountains were brought forth, or ever thou hadst formed the earth and the world, even from everlasting to everlasting, thou art God (Psalm 90:1-2 KJV).

The Lord will reign for ever and ever (Exodus 15:18).

The LORD is King for ever and ever (Psalm 10:16).

Abraham planted a tamarisk tree in Beersheba, and there he called upon the name of the LORD, the Eternal God (Genesis 21:33).

The eternal God is your refuge, and underneath are the everlasting arms. He will drive out your enemy before you, saying, 'Destroy him!' (Deuteronomy 33:27).

He stood, and shook the earth; he looked, and made the nations tremble. The ancient mountains crumbled and the age-old hills collapsed. His ways are eternal (Habakkuk 3:6).

Read Revelation 4:9-11 and Romans 1:20

Summary:

1. God's power is eternal (timeless). God is timeless (Romans 1).
2. Moses and Miriam sing a song after Pharaoh's army is destroyed declaring that the Lord will rule for ever and ever (Exodus 15).
3. David declares the Lord will be King for ever and ever (Psalm 10).
4. God is on his throne in heaven and lives for ever and ever (Revelation 4).
5. God is "eternal" (Genesis 21).
6. Moses calls God eternal (Deuteronomy 33).
7. God's ways are eternal. God is eternal (timeless) (Habakkuk 3).

Why is this Important?

Without a watch or calendar, how would you tell time? You could mark each day with the rising and setting of the sun. You would watch the seasons change. You would notice how you grew bigger or older. Time does not help us understand God. God is eternal which means timeless. That is hard to understand. Here are five things we know about God and time because He told us.

1. God does not have a beginning or an end. Everything around us has a beginning or an end. We study history to learn when things began and ended. We can plan next Saturday because time is predictable.
2. We measure everything in time. We ask, "How long have you lived here?" "When is your birthday?" God cannot be measured by time.
3. God does not grow older or bigger. We do. We celebrate birthdays and praise children as they grow up. God has never changed his age or his size.
4. God lives where time does not exist. The sun does not rise or set in space. Astronauts must eat and sleep as usual so they don't become disoriented.
5. God works where a thousand years is like a day. We honor those who live over 100 years. The United States is just over 200 years old.
God invites us to live where He lives when He offers eternal life. Only one who is eternal can offer eternal life. God is timeless. I look forward to living with Him.

Something to Do:

- Count the clocks and calendars in your home. Why do you have so many?
- Count how many times in one day someone near you says, "hurry" or gets in a hurry.
- Why does time seem to pass so slowly when doing homework and so quickly when taking a nap?
- Turn on a tap slowly. Fill a glass with water one drop at a time. Each drop represents a year. How many years pass before the glass is full? Pretend you and the world live inside the glass and God lives outside. In a similar way, God is not subject to time like we are. He has no beginning or end.

Something to Think About:

- Could you save a day by turning your clock back 24 hours?
- If you had to give up clocks or calendars, which would you choose and why?
- If you could have more time each day, how would you choose to use it?
- If you knew you had 1 day, 1 month, or 1 year to live, what special things would you do? Would you try to improve your relationship with God? How?

32. God is Trinity

What did the writing mean? We were gazing at the Mosque of Omar. A Mosque is the place where Moslems worship. The Mosque of Omar sits on top of a hill in the center of old Jerusalem. The Moslems built it where the Old Testament Temple used to stand. This Mosque is the Moslem's second most holy site. The Temple site is the most holy site to the Jews. Christians love the Temple site because Jesus taught there and promised to return there.

So what did the writing mean? The huge Arabic letters flowed around the top of the Mosque. The guide read the inscription for us, "Say not that Jesus is God's son, say only he is a prophet."

Why would the builders put a message about Jesus on their Mosque? The answer is simple. Mohammed only claimed to be God's prophet while Jesus claimed to be God's Son.

The words of the Son of God would clearly be more important than a prophet's words. Moslems and Jews know that Jesus made Himself equal with God when He claimed to be God's Son. Jesus also claimed the Holy Spirit was equal with Himself and God. That is why Christians believe in a "Trinity".

Trinity is the most difficult and mysterious of all the words we use to describe God. We use this word because it best summarizes how God talks about Himself in the Bible. God describes Himself as trinity whether anyone believes it or not. This one word divides a Christian from a faithful Moslem or an Orthodox Jew.

Where is that found in the Bible?

Therefore go and make disciples of all nations, baptizing them in the name of the Father and of the Son and of the Holy Spirit (Matthew 28:19).

May the grace of the Lord Jesus Christ, and the love of God, and the fellowship of the Holy Spirit be with you all (2 Corinthians 13:14).

Then I heard the voice of the Lord saying, "Whom shall I send? And who will go for us?" And I said, "Here am I. Send me!" (Isaiah 6:8).

Then God said, "Let us make man in our image, in our likeness, and let them rule over the fish of the sea and the birds of the air, over the livestock, over all the earth, and over all the creatures that move along the ground" (Genesis 1:26).

Summary:

1. Jesus tells the disciples to baptize in "the name" not "names". Then Jesus mentions The Father, The Son, and The Holy Spirit. You could read this verse: "...baptize in the name of the Father, Son, Holy Spirit."
2. Paul's blessing of the Corinthian church includes all three names (No blessing in the N.T. ever includes an angel or any dead human being).
3. Isaiah quotes God as saying "who will go for Us". You would expect God to say "me". God is referring to all the members of the Trinity.
4. Moses also uses a plural rather than a singular reference to God when describing God's decision to create man.

Why is this Important?

Have you ever thought so hard your head hurt? My cousin Jesse did. She told me so. Thinking about God as Trinity may make your head hurt.

In Matthew 28, Jesus taught us to baptize in the name of the Father, the Son and of the Holy Spirit. We baptize in one name (not names) but three persons are mentioned. Is your head starting to hurt?

When I add 1+1+1, that always equals 3! Yet these come under one name. Because we have one name and three persons we use the word "trinity". This is a puzzle we cannot solve with human reason. My head really hurts now.

We must admit we cannot explain the mystery. Many things about God cannot be explained. That should not really surprise you or me. My tiny mind cannot explain many things in life.

We should describe God the way He describes Himself. Make no mistake, the Bible is very clear. The Father is God, the Son is God and the Holy Spirit is God, and there is only one God. That is what we mean when we say Trinity.

Because God is Trinity, He shows us how to live in a perfect relationship. God the Father, God the Son and God the Holy Spirit all love one another all the time. They invite us to love each other the same way. Without the Trinity, we would not have this perfect example of love.

Something to Do:

• Ask two friends or your brother and sister to help you for thirty minutes. Stand back to back and join arms. For the next thirty minutes you must act as one. Any person in the family may speak to you but only one may answer. No matter what one commits to do, all must do it.

Something to think about:

• How long did you last before someone complained?

• How hard was it to still like the other two people after thirty minutes?

• Did anyone try to take charge of the group without permission from the other two?

• Would you be impressed with three people who could live like this for a whole day? A month? Would you be surprised if they still loved each other?

33. God is Truth

We were enjoying our second trip to Israel. I was too excited on the first trip to enjoy everything. This time I had to settle down. I wanted to live out a small dream.

Our bus would stop that night in Galilee. The little lake called the Sea of Galilee had not changed since the days of Jesus. Men still made their living from fishing that lake. As long as I could remember I loved to fish. As a Bible teacher, I read every story in the Bible about fishing with great interest. I told our guide how much I wanted to catch a fish from Galilee. He stopped the bus at a small store and bought some line, a hook and a few small weights.

In America I fished with my line attached to a rod and reel. In Galilee you hold the line in your hands. No rod and no reel. Fishing with a hand line would challenge me. I asked what the local men used for bait. The guide said to roll some bread into small balls and put it on the hook.

The night was dark and the gentle breeze whispered across the lake. There I was, fishing on Galilee like Peter, Andrew, James and John had done centuries before.

The little fish were quick. They ate my bait again and again. Finally I hooked a small one and brought him in. My wife took my picture. I'm prouder of that little fish than all the big fish I've caught in my life.

I've quit telling people my fishing stories. Everyone expects a fisherman to lie. In fact, my sister-in-law hung a sign in my office which reads, "I fish therefore I lie". I hope she was just teasing.

God is just the opposite. God never lies. God cannot lie because he is truth.

God's sign should read, "I'm God therefore I tell the truth".

Where is this found in the Bible?

Into your hands I commit my spirit; redeem me, O LORD, the God of truth (Psalm 31:5).
Sanctify them by the truth; your word is truth (John 17:17).

Read Isaiah 45:19

Summary:

- The Psalm writer tells us that God is truth.
- Isaiah quotes God who says He tells the truth.
- Jesus says everyone who wants to worship God must worship him in truth. Jesus claims that God's word is truth (John 17).

Why is this Important?

My mother warned me not to lie. She said, "if you lie and I find out I will not know whether you're telling the truth the next time. I won't trust your word." When my mother suspected I was not telling the truth, she would say, "I think your nose is getting longer." Of course she was referring to Pinocchio. Every time he told a lie his nose got longer and longer.

Have you ever wondered what the world would be like if people could not lie? Imagine a policeman suspects that a person stole candy from a store. He asks, "Did you take the candy?" When the person says no, he lets him go. They did not lie because they could not lie. If the person took the candy, they would have to say, "yes" even if they wanted to say, "no".

One day everyone will stand before God and tell the truth. Some people will not be embarrassed since they always told the truth. Others will have covered up their sins by telling lies, but God will know. He knows the truth. He is the truth.

Telling the truth began with God. He always told the truth. He never told a lie. He will never tell a lie. He cannot lie. When God tells us something about Himself in the Bible, we know its true even if we do not understand it. When God tells us something about ourselves, we know it is true even if we do not want to believe it. God is truth. We can trust Him. We can trust His word. God is truth.

Something to Do:

- Assume you had the same problem as Pinocchio and your nose would grow a bit longer each time you told a lie. Keep a simple record for a whole day and a whole week.
- Then, make a clay model of your nose after one day and one week.
- What would you look like after a year?
- Add up the length at the end of the day and the end of the week.

Something to Think About:

- What makes us afraid to tell the truth sometimes?
- Can we trust God to tell us the truth about eternal life, heaven, and hell?
- Can you remember a time when you really wanted people to believe you were telling the truth but they doubted you?
- Why do you think people doubt that God is telling the truth?

34. God is Unique

From my earliest memories in Missouri to my Christmas breaks in New Mexico, I loved riding my sled down snowy hills. The bigger the hill, the longer the ride. I loved them all. This winter we were visiting Colorado. My parents suggested I try skiing. "You like sledding, you'll like skiing," they said. That sounded reasonable to me. My ride up the hill was pleasant. My ride down ended in the cold snow with my right foot almost touching my ear.

I could not move. I lay there getting colder and colder hoping someone would find me. I was really glad when the ski patrol came and carried me off the hill.

During that whole time, I never thought about how unique the snowflakes were. Scientists tell us that each snowflake on that mountain was unique. There may have been "bazillions" of snowflakes on that mountain. I personally crushed at least one "bazillion" when I fell. Yet each one is unique. No two are alike.

I didn't care at the time. Since that day I've tried to spend as little time as possible in the snow! That was both my first and my last ski trip.

In one way, God is like a snowflake because He is unique. Nothing is exactly like God. I have used many things in this book to describe God and He is like all of them in small ways. But He is not like any of them completely. God is unique.

We face a big problem when we describe God. No one is exactly like Him. Nothing is exactly like Him. No combination of people or things is exactly like Him. God is unique.

Where is this found in the Bible?

"Who among the gods is like you, O LORD? Who is like you— majestic in holiness, awesome in glory, working wonders? (Exodus 15:11).

My whole being will exclaim, "Who is like you, O LORD? You rescue the poor from those too strong for them, the poor and needy from those who rob them" (Psalm 35:10).

For who in the skies above can compare with the LORD? Who is like the LORD among the heavenly beings? In the council of the holy ones God is greatly feared; he is more awesome than all who surround him. O LORD God Almighty, who is like you? You are mighty, O LORD, and your faithfulness surrounds you (Psalm 89:6-8).

Who is like the LORD our God, the One who sits enthroned on high, who stoops down to look on the heavens and the earth? (Psalm 113:5-6).

Read Isaiah 40:18 and 25-26

Summary:

1. No false god compares with the Living God (Exodus 15).
2. It's amazing that our God is a God for the poor and helpless and not just the rich and powerful (Psalm 35).
3. God, the huge God of space, takes time to look at the stars and earth (Psalm 8).
4. We do not have anything to compare with God (Isaiah 40).
5. If you were to look at everything in heaven you would find no one like God (Psalm 113).
6. God has given a name to every star. Scientists cannot even count them all (Isaiah 40).

Why is this Important?

God is everything the Bible says. He is everything at the same time. He is everything at the same time perfectly. He is everything at the same time perfectly and much more.

The most difficult thing about God was clearly seen by Isaiah. We do not have anything to compare with God. My stories in this book may help, but God is so much more than my stories or explanations. Even if we combined all the verses in the Bible, our minds could not form an adequate picture of God.

I want to help you learn to love God. You cannot love someone you do not know. I hope each chapter will help you know a little more about God. This may help you on your journey toward loving God.

Those who have given their lives to studying the Bible and learning about God admit they know so little. You have begun your learning about God. Now you must continue. There is no one as wonderful as God. There is no one like God. There is no one more worthy of your love than God. May your love for Him grow deeper every day.

He does not look like man or beast. We do not have enough words to accurately describe Him. While each snowflake is different from the next, still it is a snowflake and there are "bazillions" of them. The God of the Bible is the only true God. Any other god is a false god and not a god at all. God is the only God.

Something to Do:

- Can you find a picture of a snowflake in a book or magazine? Now see if you can draw one a little different from the picture. Cut it out and put it somewhere in your room to remind you how unique God is.

Something to Think About:

- How will you describe God since you have never seen Him?
- How many things do you know about God so far?
- Could you use all of them to describe Him to a friend? Try it.
- Have you ever wondered why people often made gods who looked like humans or animals?
- What do you think about people who worshipped gods like the sun, or wind, or fire?
- They knew they had to worship, but they did not know of the one true God. You can read about their struggle in Romans 1.

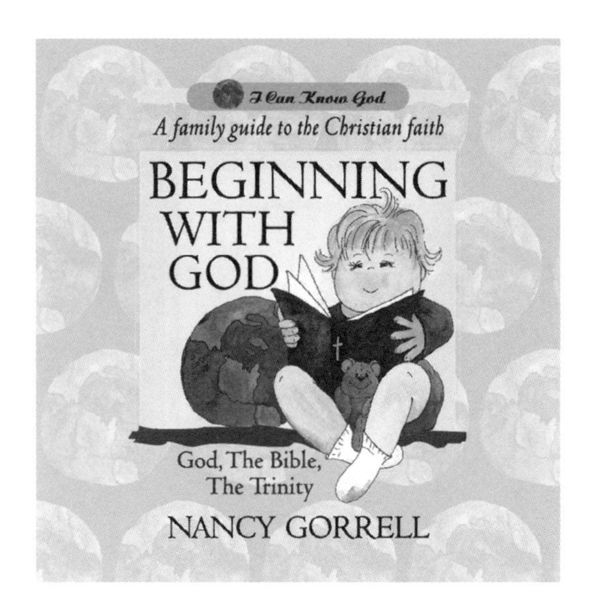

Beginning With God

God, the Bible and the Trinity
ISBN: 978-1-85792-453-4

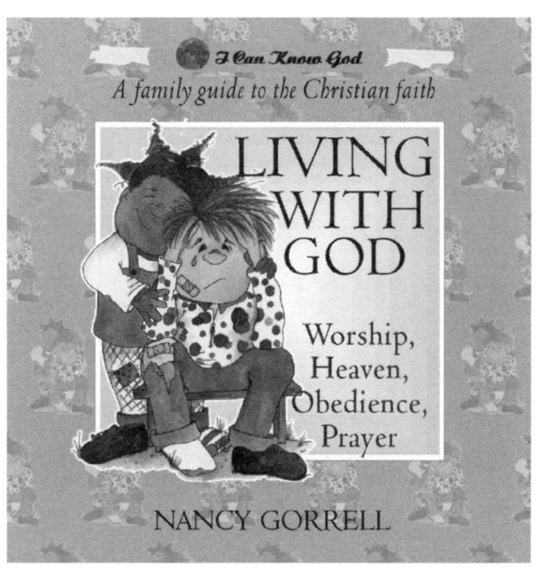

Living With God

Worship, Heaven, Obedience and Prayer
ISBN: 978-1-85792-532-6

Meeting with God

Creation, Jesus and Salvation
ISBN: 978-1-85792-531-9

Three books by author Nancy Gorrell to help parents teach young children important Christian theology and doctrine. Lively and engaging illustrations with attractively written explanations.

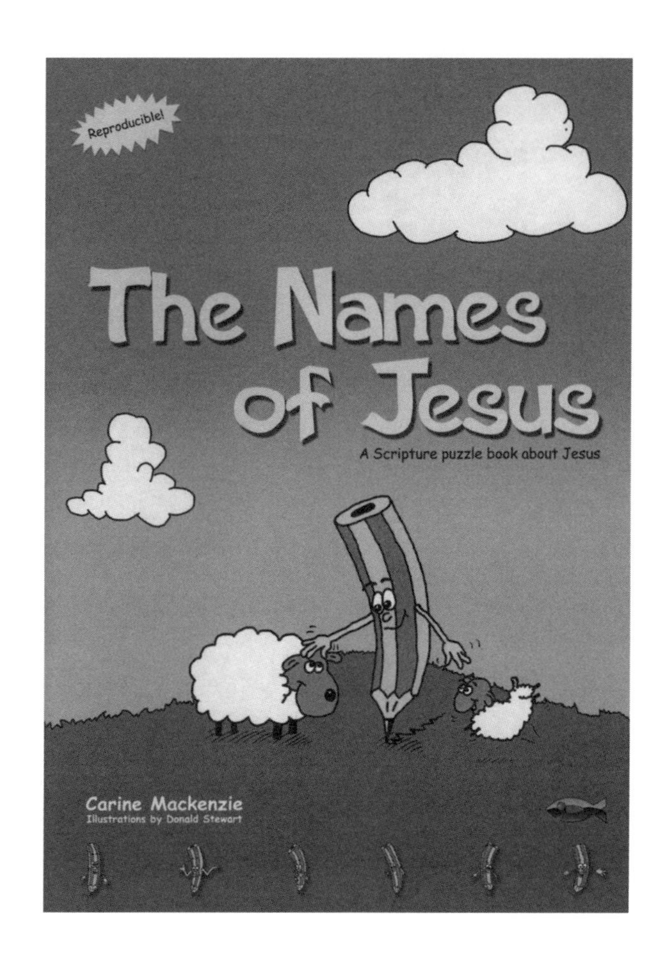

The Names of Jesus
Carine Mackenzie

This fully reproducible puzzle and work book is fun and creative. Children will find hours of entertainment and good biblical instruction about the person of Christ.

ISBN: 978-1-85792-650-7

The Big Book of Questions and Answers
Sinclair Ferguson

A book for families to discover the key doctrines of Christianity in a way that stimulates discussion and helps children want to know more.
Winner of Christian Children's Book of the Year.

ISBN: 978-1-85792-295-0

The Big Book of Questions and Answers about Jesus
Sinclair Ferguson

This book focusses on the person and work of Jesus. A great resource for parents and teachers. Shortlisted for Christian Children's Book of the Year.

ISBN: 978-1-85792-559-3

Read with Me
Jean Stapleton

A book for families to read together. Go through the whole of the Bible in a year with short and concise scripture explanations along with recommended readings. There are short sentences for new readers to get their teeth into as well as question and fact sections.

ISBN: 978-1-84550-148-8

Christian Focus Publications publishes books for adults and children under its four main imprints: Christian Focus, CF4K, Mentor and Christian Heritage. Our books reflect that God's word is reliable and Jesus is the way to know him, and live for ever with him.

Our children's publication list includes a Sunday school curriculum that covers pre-school to early teens; puzzle and activity books. We also publish personal and family devotional titles, biographies and inspirational stories that children will love.

If you are looking for quality Bible teaching for children then we have an excellent range of Bible story and age specific theological books.

From pre-school to teenage fiction, we have it covered!

Find us at our web page:
www.christianfocus.com